Second Chance

Linda Kepner

CRIMSON
ROMANCE
Avon, Massachusetts

Published by
Crimson Romance
an imprint of F+W Media, Inc.
10151 Carver Road, Suite 200
Blue Ash, Ohio 45242

www.crimsonromance.com

Copyright © 2012 by Linda Kepner

ISBN 10: 1-4405-4529-4
ISBN 13:978-1-4405-4529-0
eISBN 10: 1-4405-4528-6
eISBN 13: 978-1-4405-4528-3

Chapter 1

Dr. Roth thought this class was tedious, and hated teaching it. However his graduate assistant, Bishou Howard, loved the practice. An aspiring woman professor needed all the practice she could get, Bishou reasoned. It might be 1969 and an age of feminism, but it was still a man's world out there. It was a pleasure to have an advisor like Raymond Roth, who had a sense of humor as well as intelligence. A potentially adversarial relationship had easily become a friendship. Thus, Bishou Howard taught Introduction to World Literature 101 to incoming freshmen at East Virginia University—trying to make it interesting enough to keep a few sheep in the fold once the required courses were out of the way—while researching her PhD thesis on the theme "Passion in Literature." This gave Dr. Roth time to do reading and research, with occasional spot-checks on his only graduate assistant.

Two hundred freshman students sat in this lecture hall, and Bishou could easily see what they called in Boston "light dawning on Marble Head" as she made her points and parallels, and asked questions to make them think. Many teachers didn't allow a lecture to be interrupted, but Bishou pointed to students and asked questions to which she expected answers.

She dismissed her students and they gathered up their books. That was a sign of attention, as she well knew. They had been absorbed enough, or cautious enough, to refrain from slamming their piles of books together just because it was getting close to the end of the hour.

Dr. Roth dodged exiting students and stepped down to the center well from which Bishou taught. She nodded her greetings as she collected her notes from the lectern.

"Hey, Chief, what's on your mind?" she said cheerfully.

"The dean spoke to me today about someone who might need a little tutoring. It's a bit unusual, and I think a little confidential. Got a minute?"

"Umm, hmm," she hedged. "Got an appointment with the Rare Books Librarian. He's trying to dredge up something for me."

"Sandy's taking Roger to orientation night at the junior high, and I'm on my own tonight." Bishou had supped with the professor, his wife, and son many nights. "Cocktails at your place later?"

"Sure, if your definition of 'cocktails' includes cheap Chardonnay, which is all I've got."

Roth smiled. "My definition of 'cocktails' includes anything I don't have to pay for. I'll bring some appetizers."

"Now, that sounds good," she laughed. "I'll be back at my apartment around five."

Bishou had a minuscule apartment on the very edge of campus, close enough to the library to be useful, far enough from the lecture halls to give her some exercise each day. Sitting in an easy chair next to an unmatched couch and lounge chair, Dr. Raymond Roth eyed the books, typewriter, and study table approvingly.

"People looking at this flat would know you were a grad student. Although, admittedly, they might not be able to tell which sex."

"Which is as it should be," Bishou agreed with a laugh. She handed a glass of wine to him, while he shook crackers and cheese cubes from a paper bag onto a plate. "The height of academic luxury."

"Here's to it," he said, and they clinked wineglasses.

She sipped the Chardonnay and found it good. "What's the tutoring about? I'm kinda stretched, Dr. Roth. Do you owe Dean Clements a favor, or something?"

"No, no. It would be for actual money. I think it's the Dean who owes the President a favor."

"Come again?" She blinked.

"Well, you know this World Tobacco Conference the University has been setting up," Roth began.

"Goodness, who doesn't? It's been the only topic of the school newsletter for months. Oh, let me guess. *On parle français seulement.*"

"Well, *pas seulement.* Apparently they've got someone coming whom they didn't expect, and he might need a little tutoring in English. I'm not sure of his background—the President didn't tell the Dean—but there's something odd."

Bishou frowned. "Odd how?"

"I don't know. Something about his passport or visa."

"French colonial, maybe? When you say 'French' and 'tobacco' I think Africa."

"That might be it, but I'm not sure. Anyway, your name came up because of your French Canadian family and your Parisian studies, and Dean Clements nobly volunteered you," Roth said dryly.

"We both must remember to thank him," said Bishou, deliberately keeping any editorial tone out of her voice. After all, she was a student. She never forgot that things like this, little comments, might come back to bite her.

"Mmm. Well. Since it's a conference, there's conference money there, some of which can be used to pay an English tutor. Might not be much, but it's pocket money, Bishou."

She nodded. "Income instead of outgo. Do you know anything about this unexpected someone?"

Roth pulled a piece of paper out of his pocket. "Only his name. Louis Dessant."

"Dessant like the cigarettes?"

"That's all I know."

Bishou whistled. "That's like saying R.J. Reynolds here, Dr. Roth."

"Really?"

"Yeah. Dessant is tobacco big time. I think the cigarettes come from Réunion Island, maybe, near Madagascar in the Indian Ocean. Sort of like Hawaii for Frenchmen."

"I might have the name wrong," Roth warned. "What's the frown for?"

"I think I read something about a Dessant, in the news, maybe a year or two ago." She tried to remember, but failed. "Family scandal or something."

"Then that's probably our fellow," said Roth. "Heaven forbid any parent send us a student who isn't in trouble somewhere else." Again, they both laughed at the inevitable fact of life, and returned to the wine and cheese.

A few moments later, however, Dr. Roth grew a little more serious. "I know I'm preaching to the choir, Bishou. You've been negotiating academic landmines all your life. But if this fellow is—rather, I mean to say, if you sense some kind of trouble with him—you must tell me up front, and not try to soldier on through. When you receive your doctorate from here, you'll be only the third woman to do so in EVU history, and," he paused and cleared his throat, "that means people tend to watch what you are up to."

Equally seriously, Bishou said, "Both of us. You took me on."

"I know. I won't rehash everything we've said before. After all, we both know what we've said and done, and—knock on wood," he rapped on the rickety little end table, "we're turning into a pretty good prototype for advisor-advisee relationships for female PhD students."

"Amen, Lord," she said wryly, and they both chuckled.

"I'm just a little concerned that the dean is a little concerned, if you see what I mean. This isn't just a student whose transcripts we can look up. He's a businessman at a seminar."

"We're only talking two weeks," said Bishou. "Relax, Dr. Roth. We'll take it easy."

"It's early days," Dr. Roth observed. "We'll see."

Chapter 2

East Virginia University was a perfectly logical place to hold a tobacco-growers' conference, Bishou mused the next day as she walked to the Medlin Conference Center after her morning class and tuition sessions. And certainly a world tobacco-growers' conference. Most of the money behind the university was tobacco money. They were situated in the heart of tobacco country, a great place for tours. The university's Ag Department had done a lot of tobacco research, and was forward thinking in the face of medical discouragement about the health dangers of tobacco. She frowned wryly. And in the rear guard as far as women's rights were concerned.

A female teacher was still expected to wear high heels and stockings here, and always to appear well-groomed. Bishou had short dark hair, clear light skin with dark features, grey eyes, and a decent healthy body. She had seen women almost walk into walls admiring her "twin" brother Bat, so she supposed she wasn't bad-looking either. She could deal with stockings and high heels.

Wonder how Bat's adjusting to having me so far away from New England, she thought. *I miss them all, even our annoying parents. But there's no going back. Thank God Bat is there for our brothers, at least.* She shook her head. *Save dreaming for another day, Bishou,* she reminded herself. *It's time for the men's world of tobacco.*

She walked up to the registration table for the conference, where she saw two women and three men. A young Twiggy look-alike with short blond hair and scared-raccoon mascara looked up from her seat inquiringly.

"Hello. I'm Bishou Howard from the university. I'm supposed to be sitting in on some of this, and assisting French-speaking members of the conference."

"The current speaker is just starting," said the blond woman.

However, the other woman said, "I'm sorry, but you can't enter without a badge."

"What must I do to get one?" Bishou asked.

"Register."

"Register, as in money? Excuse me, I was asked to help. I'm not registering for this conference."

"I'm sorry," the woman said firmly. "You cannot enter the conference without a badge."

Familiar with this combat routine, Bishou simply smiled and shrugged. "Thank you, you just made my day easier. I won't attend, then. Be sure you inform President Lanthier that you turned me away, and why. I'll inform my department head as well."

"Wait a minute, wait a minute," a nearby man drawled. "Annie, if we asked the university for an interpreter for a World Tobacco Conference, we don't turn 'er away because she won't pay a fee to get in. What are you thinking?"

"No registration, no attendance," said the woman firmly.

"Fine by me," Bishou agreed, in that same pleasant voice. "I'm overworked anyway."

The man had a very pleasing accent—North Carolina, she'd bet. He simply picked up a marker and said, "What's your name, honey?"

"Bishou Howard. B-I-S-H-O-U."

That made him laugh. "I thought they said the man's name was Bishop."

She laughed, too. "No, Bishou. It's French for 'unexpected.' "

Now they all laughed, no hard feelings. "And you are," said the man. "I was expecting a Frenchman named Bishop, and I got a Frenchwoman named Bishou."

"Worse than that," she agreed humorously. "I'm a Yankee. But this is such a fine university, I wanted to come here for my studies." She had said that same line so many times, and always got the same benevolent reaction.

"I'm Gray Jackson." He put a hand on her shoulder. "Come up here, honey, and I'll try to point out Monsieur Dessant for you."

A real feminist would have broken his wrist, but Bishou filed it with all the other sexisms she encountered in a day's work, and responded to the content rather than the form. "Good, thanks. That would be a start."

They climbed a stairway to the balcony level. They looked down on five hundred men at long concentric desks, all taking notes about tobacco infections. Occasionally Bishou noticed a woman, understood to be someone's secretary, taking notes while the man next to her did not.

"One-two-three-four-five levels up from the bottom," Gray Jackson murmured in her ear, pointing. He leaned in. She could smell cologne and the inevitable cigarettes.

She murmured in return, "End chair empty, second chair in? White suit?"

"That's him." He squeezed her arm before she nodded, and let go of her. *When you're a woman,* she thought, *even academia requires a lot of body contact.*

Quietly, Bishou stepped down to that desk level, and took the idle chair. She had time to observe the stranger as she descended. She was a little surprised at what she saw. He wore a light suit with an off-white shirt and white tie, very much the Caucasian tropical gentleman. He had dark, wavy hair and dark eyebrows. But he was no spring chicken—in his mid-thirties, maybe. A pair of attractive dark eyes glanced up at her as she took the seat—and admittedly, stared for a moment. *Not my looks,* she thought, *it's the fact that I'm joining a men's conference.* His gaze returned to the speaker while she got out her pen and notebook.

She touched his elbow. The brown eyes flitted to her, inquiringly. She touched her name badge to introduce herself silently. He got it, and smiled. He touched his own badge—LOUIS DESSANT—and his lips moved equally silently to say, "*Bonjour.*" Then they both turned their attention to the speaker.

Louis had made marginal notes, both in English and French, on the preprinted note sheets the attendees had been given. That was a good idea, she thought approvingly, making up notes ahead of time for men who probably didn't spend much time in classrooms. In one corner, in lovely handwriting, he had written "Tobacco Bores?" She reached over to write *"Larves de tabac"* beneath it. He looked at it, at her. Then his face lit up as he smiled at her in relief and understanding.

Bishou felt her heart pound, and thought, *Wow.* Her gaze returned to her own papers. She told herself, *Shove it down, Howard, he's a student and you're the advisor, and you can't afford to screw this up.* She took a deep breath and fastened her gaze on the speaker instead.

It was interesting. The speaker was an ag scientist from the local federal research station, who had made a study of tobacco infestations. He spoke on methods of minimizing the effects. Louis was all attention during the talk; apparently it was a problem close to home. When the question-and-answer session began, Louis could not hear a voice speaking from the rear and hissed in frustration.

Bishou raised her hand. The speaker looked past her to a man from elsewhere, so she raised her voice instead, "Could you repeat the question, please? We can't hear it up front."

There was nothing weak about Bishou's voice; she'd spoken in this lecture hall before. But the speaker jumped a yard. The question was repeated, and the speaker replied. Bishou saw a smile in Louis's eyes, though not on his lips. *This man doesn't laugh much*, she thought.

He scribbled hurriedly on her notebook. Bishou smelled faint cologne, and cigarettes. She read his French, frowning, and raised her hand. The speaker, who was learning to ignore her at his peril, spoke to her. "Not loud enough, Miss?"

Bishou never took offense at this sort of thing, but laughed instead. "I'm sorry, Dr. Gardiner. I'm asking a question on behalf of Monsieur Dessant." She indicated the man beside her.

Immediately the speaker looked interested. "Dessant as in Dessant Cigarettes?"

Louis Dessant smiled. "Yes, as in Dessant Cigarettes. My question is complicated, so I wrote it down." His English was understandable and his voice pleasing to the ear.

"I'm trying," Bishou said, reading the note carefully. "So, Dr. Gardiner, you are saying that one should not eliminate the rust by—using the machete, dropping the leaves to the ground—that the dead leaves still harbor the rust? And it is better to apply the antibiotic to prevent the rust's return?"

"Yes, I am." Dr. Gardiner had snapped back to the topic at hand.

"But the dead leaves are there. Should they be carted away—does it go back into the soil?" She concentrated on Louis's handwriting. "If we cart the sick leaves away we run the risk that someone else will be marketing cigarettes made with Dessant tobacco, do you see? The dead, sick leaves. And that will leave us with legal issues, at least."

That opened up a whole new topic, apparently, pirate tobacco. There were strong feelings in the room. Bishou became absorbed in writing down phrases in English, explaining quickly in an undertone when she saw Louis Dessant shake his head in frustration, and translating his answers back into English when he muttered quickly to her.

He took on some of the replies himself, which surprised her. "I know that this is not a session on legal issues, that comes later in the conference," he said, in that same pleasing, very-French-accented voice. "But we cannot divorce—divide—the legal issues of making tobacco products from sick plants from making tobacco products with well plants, can we?"

"You had an incident of that, on Réunion, did you not?" asked Dr. Gardiner.

"*Oui*, and it has taken Etien and me many years for our lawyers to deal with it. The dump we used was being raided by ex-employees who had become pirate cigarette traders. They had the skills, you see, from working for us, and they—"He turned to Bishou and muttered, "*necrophagé.*"

"Scavenged," she supplied.

"Thank you. Scavenged from our dumps."

"Are the dumps better guarded now?" someone asked wryly.

"*Bien sûr*. We think. But we do not know. And there is that risk. And the dump now costs us three times as much as previously to maintain."

"The dump," someone muttered. "Gawd, I never thought of that."

Bishou's teacher-sense told her that this was turning into a good, interactive conference. Apparently, Dr. Gardiner thought the same thing. There was some more discussion, some more give-and-take, among the conference members.

Then Dr. Gardiner announced, "We're going to take a coffee break, and you can discuss this outside. It will give you an opportunity to meet each other. Then we'll come back to our next speaker, James Mandel from R.J. Reynolds, on the business of agriculture. Twenty minutes, everyone, then, back to your desks."

People stood up. In French, Louis Dessant asked Bishou, "Now what?"

"A cup of coffee and a trip to the bathroom," she replied, standing.

"Mmph." He stood, too, and felt in his pockets. "I don't know what I have for change."

"Guests of the university get their coffee for free," Bishou replied. "There should be a coffee cart in the lobby."

He looked at her in surprise. "Truly? I never went to university. This is all new to me."

"You surprise me," said Bishou. "Please come." *Venez, s'il vous plaît.* She said it the polite way, not *viens,* like she'd say to her brother Bat.

"*Je viens.*" I'm coming. Up the lecture hall steps, out the door, into the lobby. They followed the scent of coffee. The cart awaited. He followed her lead, getting a coffee cup, coffee, milk, sugar—and a croissant.

"Croissants! In America?"

"Not as good as the real thing," she replied, "but bearable. Do you want to take this back into the lecture hall?"

"It doesn't seem respectful. Can we find a corner out here?"

"Of course. Let's step outside."

Bishou led the way outdoors, where many of their fellow attendees sat on benches and planters and the grass. They found a space on a planter. Carefully, Louis spread out his napkin and put his cup and croissant on it. She smiled and thought, *he'd never pass for an American with that kind of carefulness.* She held onto her cup and set her cinnamon roll on a napkin on her lap.

He sipped coffee, then asked her, "How do you know French so well?"

"My mother is French-Canadian."

"Down here?"

"*Non,* I am from New England, from Boston."

"Ah, I see. And what brought you to Virginia?"

"My studies. I am working on my doctorate degree in world literature."

"You are a woman professor, then?" he asked.

"*Oui,*" she admitted with a smile. "Now, just a graduate student, tutoring and assisting undergraduate students. But soon, in another year, I will be a full-fledged college professor, a doctor of literature."

"*Merde de merde,*" he marveled. "And then what?"

"Then I will be looking for a job, like everyone else."

He smiled, for the first time—a small smile—but she felt she deserved it. Then his brown eyes changed direction, focusing on three men standing before them.

Gray Jackson was one of them. "Hello again, Bishou. Mr. Dessant, these gentlemen are from Galveston, and they're just starting a tobacco plantation on an island off the Texas coast. I said you might be a good man for them to talk to, seein' as how you run a tobacco plantation on an island yourself."

Louis motioned them to a nearby bench, and moved his materials down the planter's edge. Bishou followed suit. One of the men eyed her. "It might be a little borin' to listen to us talk tobacco shop, young lady."

"She stays with me," said Louis Dessant, "because I have hired her through the university. I am good in English much of the time, but there are words I do not know."

"Huh. I'll be darned. You're a college coed?" Gray Jackson asked her.

"No, sir, I'm a college professor."

"A lady college professor? This place has a Domestic Science school?"

She grinned. "You'd be sorry if I cooked your meal. I'm a literature professor."

"I'll be darned. I wonder if the University of Texas is doing this, training lady professors?"

Yes, they were, Bishou knew, but this was not the time to discuss it. "I'm sure they are, but I don't know much about UT."

As expected, the men turned back to Louis, to ask questions about tobacco growing, temperature, manpower, shipping, and labor.

Louis knew his stuff. Only occasionally did he need her to translate a word or idea. He had not begun his plantation; he had inherited it from his father and grandfather. He had a partner, Etien Campard, who took over much of the day-to-day operation and had wanted Louis to attend this conference. For the first time it struck Bishou as odd that Louis was here. The French tobacco-men, it seemed, didn't attend American conferences, but usually stayed home and grew tobacco.

Gradually, more from his attitude than anything spoken, Bishou also realized that Louis Dessant was here because he had paid his way—not on some kind of scholarship or grant, the way she had lived her life. And he did not consider it an unusual expenditure, to fly halfway around the world and get a hotel and pay for a university program, out of pocket. Simply put, he was extremely wealthy. So why the heck was he here, and why was the President of the University so uncomfortable about him?

They moved out of the bright sun and into the air-conditioned lecture hall. Another lecture, much like the first, but with a different speaker. This speaker talked about legalities. Health lawsuits about tobacco, which were now becoming prominent. Liability and insurance issues. Back in their seats, Louis frowned in concentration at the speaker, but it was clear this issue didn't matter to him as much as the tobacco infections did.

One of the dining halls was given over to the conference for the lunch break. It meant a brief walk across campus. They left their notes and conference packets at their desks.

As they walked, Bishou noticed something else. Louis had no interest in viewing the campus. Hard to believe that someone who hadn't gone to college, had never been to America, didn't look around him. Well, she did see his brown eyes flick briefly about. But not to move one's head—not to pay attention? Maybe she read too much, after all. Someplace she'd read about that habit of not moving one's head . . .

They arrived at the dining room reserved specifically for the World Tobacco Conference, and found seats opposite each other at a table. The smell of beef, peas, and mashed potatoes wafted about. Other men joined them, and discussed the morning's lectures. Louis mainly listened and ate, so Bishou did, too.

They went back to the afternoon breakout sessions, small-group sessions more like seminars, where they discussed various issues of interest to the tobacco industry. Again, she kept her notebook out, which Louis borrowed when he needed to write down a question or ask for an equivalent term in French. As they passed the pen and notebook back and forth, one of Bishou's suspicions was also confirmed.

As they were leaving at the end of the second session, one of the men from North Carolina, Vig Hansen, said, "My wife's been out shopping this afternoon, but we're meeting at the Rogers Steak House for supper, Dessant. You and Bishou want to come along?" He said it as ordinarily as if Bishou were the wife or girlfriend.

"Oh, I'm sorry, I can't," Bishou answered, before anyone could say anything embarrassing. "I've got school work to do—I've got an eight A.M. class, I'm afraid."

"Nor I." Louis Dessant yawned. "I am trying very hard to adjust, but I have *décalage*, what you call, jet lag. For me, it is almost midnight."

"You should have something in your stomach, Dessant," Hanson said reasonably. "Breakfast is a long way away."

Louis shrugged, and looked at Bishou. "*Quelle vous voulez faire?*" What do you want to do?

She shook her head. "Can't. I really need to do this school work," she replied in English. "I didn't tell you the whole truth. I'm not taking the class—I'm teaching it."

Louis shook his head, smiling. "There. Mademoiselle is out of it. But I can be tempted. I will go with you. I spend too much time alone."

They parted ways, and he went off with the delighted North Carolinians.

Bishou hit up the Student Union for some soda and a slice of pizza, which she ate thoughtfully. She looked at her watch. *Just*

5:30, she thought, *EVU Administration is winding down for the day. I'll walk toward the administration building and let that be my coin toss.*

She walked across the campus, toward the administration building, which housed the president's office. She met President Lanthier coming out the front door, still putting his arm in one of his topcoat sleeves. The coin had been tossed, and it came up heads.

"President Lanthier? Can you spare me just a moment? I'm sorry. It won't take long."

He stopped, then smiled at her. "Bishou Howard. How is our finest doctoral candidate doing?"

She smiled back at him. "Still hard at work and loving it, sir. Thanks for asking." Bishou grew more serious. "I wanted to ask you about the World Tobacco Conference, though."

He brightened. "How's it going? Well, I hope."

"Yes, very well. It's an extremely good conference. They're really getting into the topics, and I think that bodes well for future conferences, really. I think they like it here a lot."

"I am so glad to hear that," said the President heartily. "It's a high-profile event that gives us some very good publicity. It allows us to participate in the community, yet use our conference center and existing resources as well. Thank you for agreeing to help out Mr. Dessant, too. The World Tobacco Conference will have an even greater appeal if we can offer it regardless of nationality or language."

"I totally agree, sir. But I did want to ask you one question, before we move on."

"And that is?" he asked with a smile.

"Do you know what Mr. Dessant was in prison for?"

The President froze. He did not speak for a long moment. Then, in a very low tone, he murmured, "So that's what it was."

"You didn't know either," she said.

"I knew he had to get a special visa, and I had to report to the state police that he had arrived here safely," the President replied. "Frankly, that worried me a little. I hadn't realized I'd been so transparent."

"You weren't, sir," Bishou lied. "I just noticed Mr. Dessant's odd little mannerisms, and I wondered."

"I don't know. I presume some kind of white-collar crime, as they call it, because otherwise they wouldn't let him out of the country—that is, out of French jurisdiction."

"No, sir," said Bishou. "He has calluses. He's been at hard labor."

"Jesus God," said the President of the University. "No one ever told me that."

Bishou motioned to one of the nearby benches. They both sat.

"First," she said in the same low voice, "I want to promise you I won't make waves. I just wanted to know for myself. It'd be easier to tutor him if I knew exactly what I was up against."

The President sighed. "Bishou, I don't know."

She smiled at him. "Dr. Lanthier, I grew up in academia, you forget. This is like talking to my uncle." Uncles were younger than dads. Actually, though, Bishou had no uncles. It was from her dad's reactions that she knew the President was not telling the whole truth.

Lanthier smiled, and looked almost sheepish. Almost. "Truth is, I don't know, Bishou. What I do know," he looked for an expressive enough term, "is that, whatever happened, people over there are well-disposed toward him."

"Who contacted us, the American or the French Embassy?"

"Both of them," Lanthier said seriously. "I've got old school chums in both. He's got tremendous support. I would go on, Bishou, as if you didn't know any of this and it didn't matter. After all, the conference will be over in two weeks, and Mr. Dessant will go back to Réunion Island. None of us will ever see him again. And excuse me for saying something harsh and politically incorrect, but I'm going to say it anyway, and if a third person claims I said it, I'll lie like Ananias: Don't develop a crush on him, a handsome romantic Frenchman with a dark past, and blow off this dissertation. I've put my ass on the line for you, our third-ever woman doctoral candidate."

Bishou chuckled. "Never crossed my mind, sir. That dissertation is the most important thing in my life, and now you know it, too. And my family would come after me with weapons if I screwed it up—excuse me, sir."

President Lanthier laughed. "Your thesis is Passion in Literature," he reminded her.

"Researching it, not living it," she reminded him.

The president patted her hand, sounding relieved. "With incoming freshmen, we know what we're getting. With two-week conferences, we don't. At least they're not living on campus, they're all at the local hotels, so it's not our security issue. We feed their minds and bodies and send them elsewhere to sleep."

"And Mr. Dessant really has a pretty good grasp of English, and the Texans and North Carolinians like him," she added. "Some good networking going on there."

"I am so grateful you think like an academician, Bishou Howard," the President sighed, clasping her hand. "Thank you. Now I must run—I'm late for a dinner meeting."

"Oh, I'm sorry, sir."

"But I'm glad we had this chance to talk. This should remain confidential. Let's keep it just as low-key as we can, shall we?"

***

Dr. Roth, sitting in Bishou's decrepit armchair, whistled and took another sip of cheap Chardonnay. Of course Bishou told her advisor what the university president had said—that was only academic self-preservation.

"D'you like him, though? Dessant, I mean? Does he strike you as a decent guy?"

"Yes," said Bishou thoughtfully, "he does. And, at bottom, Lanthier really does give good advice—keep your pecker in your pocket, even if you're a girl."

"Lanthier probably wasn't aware that your brother is a Sergeant Major in the Marines, though," Roth observed wryly.

"Nor is he aware of it yet. I was polite," Bishou replied. She sniffed the aromatic bouquet of the Chardonnay—it wasn't that bad. "I said literally what I told you I said. Besides, Bat's out of it. He left the Marines after his hitch in Southeast Asia. Someone has to stay at home to take care of our brothers. Our parents can't cope with raising two boys. Bat can."

"And you're down here in Virginia." Roth shook his head. "What happens after the doctorate?"

"I look for work. Wherever it is. If it's close enough for the boys, I take one or both of them as well. That's the deal. Bat did Marines, I do doctorate, we make sure Andy and Gerry are taken care of. They're only eleven and thirteen years old. Our parents aren't gaga, Dr. Roth, far from it—but, to put it nicely, sometimes they have unrealistic expectations from life. Mom's already in a wheelchair, too."

"You and Bat are the real parents."

She nodded. "It's always been that way. We're used to checkbook balancing, oil changes, insurance papers, house painting, road trips, all that jazz." She smiled. "Our family is very labor-intensive, but it's fun."

"I'll take your word for it. So what about Louis Dessant?"

"I'm dreadfully curious, Dr. Roth. And I do feel that I could instruct him better if I knew where he was coming from. But at the same time—do you think I'm just giving in to feminine curiosity?"

"Hell, no," said Roth. "Now I'm wondering, too."

"Maybe there are some ways to find out that aren't quite as—direct—as just coming out and asking Mr. Dessant," Bishou said. "I've got the feeling this is not a topic he wants to discuss."

"Well, no wonder. But if you invite him out to dinner and start pumping him, every gossip on campus is going to talk about you, believe me. You know what this community can be like."

"I'll watch it," said Bishou. "I'll do my research under the table."

"I think it would be wise," said Dr. Roth.

Chapter 3

Bishou taught her 8:00 Intro to World Literature class. By 9:00, having lectured to three hundred freshmen, she was most definitely ready for coffee. She went to the student union, got her coffee, and checked her student mailbox. She saw a note from the interlibrary loan librarian, asking her to pick up some material she had requested. There would be a fee of $25, not the usual $3.

"That's where my money goes," she sighed, checking her wallet before she headed to the library.

An anemic young man at the interlibrary loan desk jumped up when he saw her coming. "Miss Howard, I've got those things for you."

"Thanks. What was the fee about?"

"I teletyped a request to have materials express-mailed from Paris." The cutting edge of high-tech; he was obviously proud of their work. "You're lucky the Humanities Department absorbed part of the cost."

"Yes, I am, thank God." She gave him the $25.00, and waited patiently for a receipt. After all, she would have to do her taxes later. Undergraduates without encumbrances never thought of these things.

He handed her a large, flat envelope. "*Crimes de Passion Modernes.*" His accent was horrible. "Pictures and everything."

"Really?" She opened the envelope.

"Really. Dissertation guidelines are being changed to accommodate facsimiles. They're a literal reprint of the pages in question, and they're going to be allowed in dissertations in a year or two—talks are underway." He grinned. "Probably too late for you, but not the next candidate."

"Too true. Something always changes."

The young man—a sophomore, maybe—nodded sagely. "Immutable text of dissertations, changed by time and technology. Oh, well. Hope it helps."

Bishou thanked him, and walked back out into the sunshine. She pulled out the sheets from the envelope, and froze.

Louis Dessant's picture stared up at her.

She made it to a bench before her knees gave way and read the article, slowly and incredulously. It was in French, from a major newspaper, but a feature story rather than a news article—a summary of a theme. It was dated three years ago. And yes, as the librarian had said, the title was Modern Crimes of Passion.

The caption below Louis's head-and-shoulders photo translated as, "The notorious Louis Dessant, of the Dessant Cigarette dynasty, was released from prison after the French government received clamorous support for him from the entire newly developed Overseas Department of La Réunion."

She delved further into the article, looking for Louis's name, and found it at last. "Duped into an unwitting marriage with a beautiful confidence artist, Louis Dessant murdered the private detective who pursued them throughout France. Dessant later found that his false wife had killed the mail-order bride he had actually arranged to marry on Réunion Island, and taken her place. By then, he was so deeply in love with the false Madame Dessant that he was willing to die for her, and nearly did so, allowing himself to be slowly poisoned to death in an alpine hideout. Mme. Celie Dessant (real name, Carola Christina Alese) put a gun to her head and committed suicide before her shocked husband, rather than allow the police to take her. She left him alone to face bereavement, arrest, betrayal, and a sentence of hard labor."

"Good God." Bishou's hands shook so badly she could hardly return the papers to the envelope.

She sat in the bright, warm sunshine, feeling so cold she shivered. Deeply in love. Murder. Poison. Suicide. Well, that was passion, wasn't it? That was what she was doing her thesis on— observing it, not living it. This was one hell of an observation.

She thought again of Dr. Roth, President Lanthier, even Bat. *All right,* she promised them silently, *I'm an academic and I'll behave like one, don't worry. Louis Dessant is just an interesting advisee, for two weeks only, and then he'll be gone.* Even as she said this to herself, she felt a twinge of unhappiness. She massaged her hands and feet to make the cold and numbness go away. The shock had been physical. Nothing had hit her that hard in years.

Bishou took a deep breath. *Get used to it,* she told herself. *The rest of your life is going to be like this. If you're going to be a woman professor, Howard, expect to be alone.*

As Jean-Baptiste Howard, "Bat" her brother, had warned her, you just slogged through the traumatic times until you came out the other side. In the meantime, though, you tried to be fair to everyone else, and not let your outlook spoil their lives. Like they did for their younger brothers, who didn't remember a time when their parents weren't the victims of paralysis or dementia.

She stood. All right, she could do that. Louis Dessant was probably in America, a place he'd never been, for a change of scene. The least she could do was make sure it was a good experience. *Back into the academic shell,* she told herself. *Let's go.*

They had already reached the morning coffee break when she stepped inside the Medlin Conference Center. Men sat everywhere, in the searing bright sunshine, talking and drinking coffee. She didn't see Dessant among the men outside, not on the grass or benches or planters. Then she thought, *No, he likes things more structured,* and headed for the little coffee shop in the next building.

He was alone, at a tiny table, his head resting on one hand, reading notes. He had a cup of coffee and nothing else. She thought he looked tired and discouraged.

"Monsieur Dessant?"

He looked up at her, surprised, and rose from his seat. "Mademoiselle Howard! I did not think you were coming."

"I'm sorry." Bishou sat down in the opposite seat. "I had to teach, then I had to run some errands. I hadn't meant to leave you by yourself. It's my fault."

"Oh, no, no. I expect too much." He switched from English to French as he sat down. "The first speaker was on medical and legal issues, and we have not progressed so far in France. I found it very tedious. I was just trying to find highlights to describe this to Etien when I return, in case we find ourselves with similar legal issues in the future. But I doubt it very much. I cannot imagine it happening to us."

"It's good to be prepared, though, just in case it does."

"I suppose so." Louis underlined something else on the preprinted notes. Then he looked up at her with eyes almost as tired as his photo in the news clippings. "I missed you," he said simply.

She dropped her gaze. "*Vous êtes trés gentil.*" You are very kind. "You are not eating anything. Did you have any breakfast?"

"*Non.*"

"I'll get a croissant for you." She stood, and motioned him back into his chair when he started to rise. "*Non, non,* you must eat. A student cannot concentrate when his stomach is empty."

Put that way, he acquiesced with the slightest smile. "*D'accord.*"

When she returned, Louis was not alone at the table. Vig, Gray, and another tobacco-man had found him, and were explaining in great detail how the agricultural laws affected their tobacco business. They stood and found a chair for Bishou—chivalry was not completely dead in the South—and watched as Bishou laid out the croissants, butter, and jam for Louis.

"That's the sort of lady to have, Louis," Vig commented, "one who knows the way to a man's heart is through his stomach."

Louis Dessant, buttering his croissant, gave them only a token smile. "I am not—how you said last night—shopping, my friend. My business here is tobacco only."

Vig cocked an eye at Bishou. "And you, Little Miss? No plans to marry a rich widower tobacco man, eh?"

"No plans at all to marry a rich widower tobacco-man," she concurred with a smile. "University business only."

Louis glanced at her sharply, but ate his croissant in silence. Then it was time for them to return to the lecture hall for the second morning lecture.

As they walked across the quad to the lecture hall, Louis asked her, in French, "We talked about wives at dinner last night. You were not there. How did you know I was a widower?"

"You wear no ring," Bishou replied.

"I might never have married," he demurred.

"Thirty years old, with your looks?" she said. "I think yes."

He reddened. "Thirty-five," he said, "but thank you for the compliment. I wish you had been along last night. I was the only one at their dinner without a companion."

"*Mes apologies.* But I really had to prepare for this morning's lecture."

"I understand."

She wondered if he did.

They found the same seats as the previous day, and Bishou got out her notebook. Soon she was scribbling frantically about soil nutrients and environmental damage and fertilizers, while Louis did the same, back and forth. It was a busy, purging, profitable session.

"Mr. Dessant?" The lecturer knew who he was. The foreign tobacco-man had become known.

"Is this information shared among the agricultural research centers of various governments? I had never heard this soil nutrient information before, not as research."

"I'm not sure, but I can find out for you. I know it's shared among the states of the United States, the Canadian provinces, and most of the British Commonwealth, but I don't know about the French departments, or Africa."

"Perhaps the universities?"

"Definitely the universities. You can probably find out easier than I can which university systems have pipelines into the agricultural research stations."

"That is a good thought. Thank you." He made more notes.

At lunch break, Louis said to Bishou, "You will have lunch with us?"

"Certainly," she replied, rising to accompany him. He reached for the tote bag, but she drew back. "No, no. I can carry my own things, I promise."

He inclined his head briefly. "As you wish."

They walked across campus to the reserved dining room. As they entered, they could smell beef cooking. The Texans and North Carolinians waved at them, and Louis and Bishou joined their table.

"Heeey, Bishou! Thought we lost you this morning. That tobacco was just too exciting for you, huh?" Gray Jackson greeted her.

"Not hardly." She smiled as she sat down. "I have a job, too, you know."

"I still can't get over it. A pretty thing like you, a college professor. You must be really brainy, honey," one of the other tobacco-men teased.

"It's just teaching, like anywhere else. Don't you know any women teachers?"

"Well, yeah, but not in colleges."

"Well, keep watching us women. We'll surprise you."

The men laughed. One said, "Huh. And in the meantime, there's some lonely man somewhere, who isn't being taken care of the way he should be."

"He's safer than if he were married to me," said Bishou, and the laughter started again.

They all had a good lunch, and talked tobacco and soil nutrients.

Gray Jackson said, "I hadn't thought about Réunion being a volcanic island. Do you test the soil and water regularly?"

Louis nodded. "Not only for acidity and alkalinity, but also possible volcanic activity. We have seen some smoke, some ash—not a lot—but one never knows."

"Like Hawaii?" Bishou asked him.

He agreed. "Much like Hawaii. I was interested in hearing what the Hawaiian grower had to say, but it appears he is getting ready to shut down."

"He was talkin' a lot about pineapples," another man grumbled.

"I think it is . . ." Louis said something to Bishou in French.

"The path of least resistance," she offered, as a substitute phrase.

"*Oui,* that is it, exactly. If I wanted to give up, there is always sugar cane. Our island is turning to sugar and electricity production."

"No pineapples?" asked Gray with a grin.

"Some pineapples." Louis named a prominent company. "Pineapples are their domain—a major agribusiness. It would be—what is the phrase—selling out."

"Never been tempted to sell out, yourself?" asked Vig.

"I have sold out," said Louis quietly, "and discovered I had made a serious mistake. I begged to be allowed back in the business. And here I stay. This is what I know. I won't be such a fool a second time."

Some of the men grunted approval. Bishou marveled that, under other conditions, these redneck, macho men would consider a Frenchman too effete for comfort. Yet here was Louis Dessant, speaking their language—tobacco—and admitting his own mistakes. And they were accepting him.

"What made you sell out?" Vig asked.

"My wife. She wanted to live in Paris, and living in Paris takes money."

"So you went back to the tobacco plantation after she died?" asked Gray.

"A while after, but yes."

He spoke only the truth, but now Bishou understood the meaning behind it. He never mentioned the agony and humiliation he had gone through. All he offered was a bare statement about a woman he had married. Bishou kept her eyes on her plate, and ate.

After dessert, they adjourned for a few minutes before the afternoon sessions started. Outdoors, Louis lit up a cigarette—a Dessant, of course—and inquired, "Do you smoke?"

"Not much. It bothers my throat. Usually I just steal a couple of puffs off someone else's cigarette."

He smiled, took another puff, and held the cigarette almost to her lips. She accepted, taking it from his hand. She inhaled the pleasant, distinctive fresh smoke of a Dessant cigarette. After she exhaled, she commented, "I haven't had one of these since I was in Paris, a few years ago."

"Oh? Where were you in Paris?"

"The usual tourist and student places. The Louvre, Versailles, Musée des Beaux-Arts, Notre Dame, Sacré Coeur, the Left Bank."

"We visited only the restaurants and cinemas when we were there. Were you there by yourself?"

"*Non*, my fellow students were in Paris for two weeks, and then my brother Bat came over. Bat and I spent two weeks there together."

"Bat?"

"Jean-Baptiste Howard. They call us the twins, but he is actually a year older than I am. He's my best friend."

"You are the only children?"

"Oh, *non*. We have two younger brothers as well."

"And your parents?"

"You are asking a lot of personal questions, Monsieur," Bishou said.

Louis reddened immediately. "I'm sorry. But it was only because you mentioned Paris. I did not mean to offend."

"You didn't offend." She took another puff of the cigarette he handed her, and then gave it back. "We have had trouble with our parents. My parents were in a car accident seven years ago, and my mother has been in a wheelchair ever since. Possibly it was by choice, at first, but by now, her muscles have atrophied." Bishou shrugged unhappily. "My father is more than a little eccentric, probably because of the head injuries he received then. We don't know. Sometimes it is a struggle. I wouldn't leave the boys with them if Bat wasn't there."

Louis cupped his hands around his cigarette, and focused on it carefully, not looking at her. "At least my wife and I did not have children to worry about."

"Sometimes that's a good thing."

"Yes," he said, gazing into her eyes for a moment. "I suppose so."

***

The seminars were interesting and thought-provoking, if you were a tobacco-growing man. Bishou was hard-pressed to keep up the translations. At the end of two seminars, she felt like she had just come from gym class.

In the now-empty lecture hall, an amused Louis Dessant took her papers from her and copied over some notes in his nice French handwriting. "I need to make these presentable, Mademoiselle Howard, while we still remember what they are." His gaze flicked to her face, then back to his copywork. "Tomorrow is the Wednesday break. Will you go on the tour with us? By autobus?"

"Where are you going?" she asked.

"Parts of North Carolina and Virginia. The auction barns are not yet in session, but we can see them, and they will give us tours. Vig and his family are all excited, to have us in their territory."

"I'm not surprised. Welcoming his own tribe, so to speak."

Louis chuckled. "Probably true. Would you accompany me? I will pay for your lunch, and for your autobus fare."

With anyone else, she would make a joke about a date, but she didn't feel right joking with him. "I don't have a morning lecture, but I do have tutoring sessions later in the day."

"Are you able to cancel them?" This time, he made eye contact. "Or would you rather not? I know it is arrogant of me to assume you are free."

She caught her breath again. "It's still early in the semester, so the students aren't in trouble yet. They can afford to skip tutoring sessions. I'll see what my schedule looks like."

"I will tell them you are attending, so there are enough box lunches. If you do not come, well then, the more for me, I suppose." A smile barely touched his lips. "I am getting better at the English, too, but still, it is nice for me to have someone to fall back on. I hope you can come."

"Hey, kids," Vig Hansen called from behind them. "You coming to dinner? Sukey wants to meet you, Bishou."

"Is Madame outside?" asked Louis.

"Not for another half an hour or so." The old tobacconeer eyed their paperwork. "Brushing up your notes?"

"*Oui.* I want to be able to remember tomorrow what I wrote today." Louis made another note. Then he looked at Bishou. "Well? Are you coming to dinner?"

A small note of frustration crept into her voice. "Monsieur Dessant, here are the choices. If I go to dinner with you tonight, I cannot go on the bus trip because I won't have a chance this evening to check the student schedules and cancel tutor sessions. If I go home right now and get working, I will be able to go on the bus trip and spend all day tomorrow with all of you. Which shall it be?"

Vig chuckled. Louis's eyes opened wide and looked very apologetic—yes, he was a born heartbreaker, whether he realized it or not. "I choose the autobus all day tomorrow. And I will owe you a dinner myself then."

"No, sir, you won't. I'm representing the university here, and I have to stay within the lines. I'm enjoying everyone a lot—this is a great job—but I'm still a collegiate representative and I have to behave like it. No private dinners."

"No more than if it was a man I asked?"

"That's it, exactly."

"*Bien entendu*." Louis nodded, satisfied.

"I'm gonna send Sukey in here," Vig threatened.

Louis held up a hand. "*Non, non, mon ami*. Bishou is part of our business relationship with the university."

"He's right, Mr. Hanson. I'm sorry," Bishou apologized.

Louis and Bishou gathered up their paperwork, and left the hall with Vig Hansen. At the door to the Medlin Convention Center, the men turned in one direction while Bishou turned in the other and hurried off into the darkness.

She reached the grad-student housing, unlocked the big front door, and went inside. The smells of laundry and steamy suppers filled the air. She said hello to Marie Norton, her downstairs neighbor, and climbed the stairs to her rooms. Once inside, with the door locked, Bishou looked with dismay in the mirror in her tiny bathroom. She had really wanted to go with them, but she hadn't realized she looked that sad.

Bishou was consoled to see that she had no labor-intensive students on her Wednesday schedule. She spent a few minutes writing notes to all of them saying she was unavailable today and would see them next Wednesday. Then, she took a deep breath, sat down with a fresh piece of paper, and started to write.

> *Dear Bat,*
> *Don't yell at me, please. I'm doing my best, really I am. I'm still on the straight, and staying there. But I just met the only man I would ever marry, if we both weren't trying so damn hard not to ruin our lives.*

He's a cute Frenchman, and I'm tutoring him for pay, so I have double the reason not to screw up.

He's got everything wrong with him. He's a widower, he's done time, and he was involved in a scandal. Remember when we were in Paris, the papers printed something about a crime of passion involving a member of the Dessant Cigarette family? Well, this is Louis Dessant. Triple the reason not to screw up.

But, man. Talk about my dissertation coming to life and hitting me in the face. Quadruple the reason not to screw up. Fortunately, I'm only the interpreter. Apparently, he still carries a torch for the woman who screwed him to the wall. She blew her brains out while he watched, and left him to be arrested as accessory to all her crimes. Okay, so maybe he's not smart. Or maybe it really was passion. I've heard him speak of the tobacco business, and he's got his head together on that, so I'm inclined to think it's the latter.

I never really forget you. Fair's fair. I'm doing my hitch for the doctorate, just as you did yours for the Marines, and yep, I'll come take up the slack when I'm done. But whew, this guy affects my breathing. Is it love, or just tobacco fumes?

Write back. Without yelling.

Love, Bishou

She needed a breath of fresh air and decided to walk to the campus post office with the letter and the notes to her students. But first, she changed out of her skirt and stockings, into slacks—the last thing she needed was another run in her stockings, and this was evening, her leisure time, after all—and put on her comfortable walking shoes.

It was nearly dark out, a soft warm April evening. Bishou couldn't distinguish people's faces underneath street lamps, although their hair glowed. She walked across campus on the paths, reached the post office, and popped the notes and letter in their respective slots.

Then she just walked around the campus, and thought a lot. Yes, she'd rather be at a nice dinner with some fun people—but around here, that would be a ticket for destruction. Now that she'd written Bat, she'd got it out of her system. Bat would either send fatherly advice, or else a diatribe that would scorch the paper, no telling which. But she wasn't worried about that. Bishou smiled to herself. She was in a good place in her life right now. President Lanthier and Dr. Roth were completely right. Get that sheepskin, and then the world would be her oyster. More or less. *Just don't start a tradition of blowing things.*

Chapter 4

The bus was one of the university's oldest—a flop-windowed, low-slung, green-and-blue diesel-stinking nightmare. Bishou climbed aboard, to discover Louis already had a seat for them near the rear of the bus and was waiting for her. She sidled back to him. He rose and stepped into the aisle.

"No, no, you take the window seat," she said. "You'll want to see things on this tour."

"Are you sure?" he asked, in the voice of someone who really wanted the window seat anyway.

She smiled. "Absolutely."

He didn't need much persuading to slide in. He stared out the window, looking like a kid on a school bus.

"Where on earth did they come up with this antique?" she asked.

"It looks average for my island," Louis said. "Most of ours don't even have roofs, let alone windows."

"What do you do when it rains?" she asked.

He looked at her, his eyes twinkling. "Get wet."

"I had to ask."

The bus started up. Dr. Gardiner, bus microphone in hand, was their tour guide. He pointed out the rivers, the soils, the tobacco fields, the plantations, the cotton fields, the forests and mountains as the bus rolled along slowly.

Louis Dessant was not the only kid on this school bus. The men were all talking, pointing to this and that feature. Louis took it all in. He asked questions of Vig, seated a few rows ahead of him, and Gray, in the back, and the Texans who were all over the bus. Their wives were here, too, interjecting occasional comments.

They stopped at the first tobacco plantation, got out, and walked around. For the men, it was almost a calming experience to be among tobacco leaves again after a few days in academia. Bishou

35

saw Louis stroke a tobacco plant like an old friend, and he was not the only one. The damp, almost steamy atmosphere had its own particular young-tobacco scent. From the look in the eyes of these men, their concentration, even the way they walked, this was serious business. Bishou watched the men with interest as they came to life.

Louis, deeply in conversation with a host tobacco planter, motioned her to him. "Mademoiselle, *comment dit-on 'filtre' en anglais?*"

"The same as in French," she replied, in English. "Filter."

"*Oui, merci,*" he said and continued speaking to his host.

Bishou felt someone grip her arm, and looked to see a substantial Southern lady hanging on to her. "You'd be the interpreter, then. The college professor?" she drawled.

"Yes, that's me," Bishou admitted with a smile.

"I'm Sukey Hansen. How come you didn't come to dinner last night? I wanted to meet you."

"I had to write excuses for all the courses I'm skipping today, to come on this trip," Bishou answered.

"It's nice of you to make time for Messyoour Dessant," Sukey said, "though he's awfully sweet. Definitely worth a woman's time. You known him long?"

"As long as you have," Bishou said. "I'm a paid translator from the university."

"Good golly! I didn't know that. You're doing this for money?"

"Beats waitressing."

"I suppose it does." Sukey looked impressed. "The menfolk told me you two were a couple."

"If we were a couple, I'd be fired," Bishou replied, putting it as plainly as she could manage. "It's against the rules."

"I'm sorry, honey. I was mistook. But he is cute, isn't he?"

Bishou admitted, "Yes, he is. And completely hands-off."

"That stinks," said Sukey Hansen. "I won't nudge you the way Vig wanted me to, then."

"Vig wanted you to nudge me?"

"Mmm-hmm. He said that lonely widower would fall into your arms at a touch, and that I should tell you to touch him."

"And I would be in deep shit," said Bishou.

"Mmm-hmm. Now I can tell Vig to mind his own business, with good reason. Okay, if you don't want to accept our invitations to dinner, I understand. Like matches to the kerosene. But I wish you'd come sometime, just to talk. Us womenfolk have got to stick together, you know."

Some of the other women gathered around them. They were curious about the interpreter, college professor, whatever they wanted to label Bishou. Her daily life was completely beyond the imagination of most of these women.

"You got other college professors in your family?" one woman asked her.

"Yes," Bishou said. "My father was a college professor, and my mother taught in an exclusive private school in New England."

Before the men returned from their inspections of the tobacco barns, Bishou's biography had been thoroughly brought out and examined by the women on this tour. She felt like she had passed some kind of test, or at least hadn't been thrown out of the ring.

Back in the bus, Bishou asked Louis, "Where is your jacket?"

He gestured toward the front of the bus. "Up there. It is too hot to wear it." He wore a silk shirt, decorated with small white grids and tiny colored squares. His shirt was unbuttoned at his throat, and he had rolled up the sleeves not quite to his elbows. "*La grange était comme un four.*" The barn was like an oven. He leaned back and closed his eyes.

For a few moments, Bishou regarded his handsome face, the dark brows, the closed eyes, the perfect lips. His forearms were slightly bronzed and muscular. Muscles strained against the silk shirt—no undershirt, probably. Frenchmen wouldn't wear them in the African heat. *This is like a French movie*, Bishou thought uncomfortably, *where the woman lies back seductively and waits for the man to touch her and undress her, except the roles are reversed. He may mean it or not, but if I don't find something else for my hands and eyes to do, I'm going to be in very big trouble.* For a few moments, Bishou regarded his attractive face, the dark brows, the closed eyes, the perfect lips. His forearms were slightly bronzed and muscular. Muscles strained against the silk shirt – no undershirt, probably, either. Frenchmen wouldn't want them in the African heat.

Bishou reached for her tote bag, took out one of the books she had assigned to her Intro to World Lit class, and sat back to read. She made notes in the margins, guessing where students would have problems or would miss an important point. She needed to bring these points out in her lectures. *Can't expect them to continue with their studies if you don't give them a few handholds,* she thought. Bishou glanced at Louis and realized he was sound asleep. Quietly, for another half-hour, she worked on her notes while the bus trundled down the highway.

The bus shuddered and turned down a rustic road, probably the driveway to the next stop. They arrived at a large farm. The first thing she saw was an open-air building with picnic tables in it. *Our lunch stop,* she realized. People were waiting for them. The bus vibrated to a stop in front of the group. People rose from their seats.

One of the Texans grinned at her. "Out cold, is he?"

Bishou nodded, and smiled back at him. Waking up Louis Dessant would be awkward. She grasped his shoulder, feeling silk and damp warmth. "Monsieur Dessant, *levez-vous.*" He did not respond. She shook his shoulder. "Monsieur Dessant. Louis. *Levez-vous.*"

Gray Jackson now stood in the aisle beside her, grinning. "Louis said he was having trouble sleeping in a motel room, but it doesn't seem like it's any problem at all on this old bus."

"It doesn't look that way," Bishou agreed, changing her tactic to the one that annoyed her brother the most. She stroked Louis's cheek, drawing the nails of two fingers from the corner of his mouth across the trace of dark beard—a rasping sound that could be like sandpaper to the beard's owner.

"*D'accord, d'accord, je me leve*," murmured Dessant. His eyes snapped open suddenly. He sat up in surprise as if he wondered what happened.

"Good trick," Gray chuckled.

"Three brothers," she replied.

Gray laughed out loud. "You must be an annoying kid sister."

"Yep." She stepped into the aisle in front of Gray Jackson, who placed a hand on her shoulder, as she'd expected, and drew her toward him. In turn, she reached out a hand to Louis Dessant. "Lunchtime. You coming?"

"Hmm. Mmph. Yes." Sleepily, he took her hand, but brought himself to his feet under his own power. "I was sound asleep. I was so comfortable." Seeing Gray's grasp on Bishou, he slid out in front of her, and stumbled. "I'm all right, just—how to say it—fuzzy in the thinking."

She caught him, thinking, *he's slightly smaller than my brother, a nice size*. With Louis before her, still sleepy and needing support, and Gray behind her, hand on her shoulder, she found herself thinking, *Feminism be damned, this feels normal and nice*. However, her very next thought was, *Damn, Bishou, keep your mind on your work!*

They were introduced to their hosts, then seated at the picnic tables. The lunch boxes were passed out, and iced tea was provided in paper cups.

"All you gentlemen should drink plenty of tea," Bishou said to her table full of Texans and North Carolinians. "Those hot auction barns dehydrated you more than you realize."

"You're right, I know," Louis agreed, drinking his first cupful. "I should not be minding this so much, but I have spent too long away from my island."

Seated between Louis and Gray, Bishou sipped slowly and nodded. "Tea or water—you aren't drinking enough of it. Liquor in the evening doesn't help, either. Alcohol dehydrates you."

Vig, sitting opposite them with Sukey, chuckled. "But that cold beer tastes mighty damn good, and so do the ice cubes in the bourbon." Everyone laughed. "How do you know all about dehydration, Bishou? You're a Yankee."

"My brother the Sergeant Major."

"Holy crap." Vig stared at her. "Marines?"

"Semper fi," she affirmed. "My parents may be cloud-minders, but my brother takes up the slack. He drills the family just like we were his recruits."

"I will be damned. 'Nam?"

"Two hitches. Out a year now."

"Jesus God." Gray was staring as well.

"I did not understand all of that," said Louis. "What is semper fi?"

"Semper fidelis," Vig explained to him, passing lunch boxes down the table. "Always faithful. The motto of the United States Marine Corps."

"Ah." Louis nodded. "When you said Marine, I thought—*marin*."

"I know you did," replied Bishou. "That's the most common mistake in the French language, I think. A U.S. Marine is definitely not a sailor, *un marin*. We have to watch out for dehydration in New England, too." Seeing their blank looks, she explained, "Instead of the water evaporating, it freezes. Your body still can't get water, do you see?"

Sukey stared. "I never thought of that."

"Do you hike in snow?" asked Louis.

"With a brother who's a Sergeant Major? What do you think?" she returned with a grin. "Oh, oh, he'll be after me for spending too much time sitting in classrooms and being out of shape."

Louis Dessant stared at the table, and said, "I hate snow."

"It all depends on how you're prepared for it."

"I suppose so," he said, but she noticed an unpleasant look on his face.

Louis read the handwriting on his boxed lunch. "Roast— what? Is that *biftek*?"

"Yes," she replied. "Some French words come from English. Beefsteak here, *biftek* there."

"Roast beef sandwich? Is that what you've got?" asked Sukey. "I'll be darned. Now I know a word in French."

Her comment dispelled Louis's unpleasant mood. He laughed. "You must learn more, so that you and Vig can come and visit me someday."

"Someday," she agreed, "when the kids are in college."

"As if we'll have any more money then," Vig grumbled.

Louis's eyes twinkled. He said something in French so quickly to Bishou that it took her a moment to get it. Then she started to laugh. "Monsieur Dessant says that you should visit his plantation, we'll get you a tobacco subsidy."

The table roared with laughter. Tobacco humor.

Louis laid out his food carefully; Bishou ate hers directly from the box. The EVU Food Service had come through with a pretty good lunch.

After they'd finished eating, they got back on the bus to tour the plantation, which also grew cotton. Bishou thought that was odd, but apparently Louis Dessant didn't. "They make filter cigarettes," he explained to her. "So they do not have to buy cotton from somewhere else for the filters."

"I never thought about that before," Bishou admitted.

"Mmph." It was a very French sound. He pulled out his notebook, and opened to a page where he had drawn the parts of a filtered cigarette. "I'm not sure Etien is ready for this, he is so very cautious, but I think we have to begin thinking about filter cigarettes. It is—*effeminate, comment dit-on*?"

"Sissy?" she asked, stifling laughter.

"*Oui.* Sissy, to have filters on the cigarettes, *n'est-ce pas?* But I think women will want them more, and health issues will make them—more prominent, that is the word I want."

"You might have something there."

"I have been thinking about it all through this conference." He made a note on his page with the cigarette drawing. "But machines must be modified, and I am not sure there are any French manufacturers making what we need for a filter cigarette. Then there is the promotion and marketing. I am not sure Etien is brave enough to risk it."

"Are you?" she asked.

"I take risks."

"Suppose it doesn't work?"

"Then I look stupid. Not for the first time. But it is my name on the package, not Etien's."

"You're very brave."

For the first time, she saw a smile touch both Louis's eyes and lips. "*Non,* I am stubborn. And, as I said, it is my name on the package." He leaned back in his seat, stared toward the roof, and sighed. "I might be wrong. If I am, I take responsibility for my mistakes. Not for the first time."

"Do you have to consult with the rest of the Dessant family, like so many of these tobacco families do?"

"There is no family," Louis Dessant said. "I am the last."

"Oh," she apologized, "I'm sorry. I was rude."

He patted her hand. "*De rien.* The Campards inherit everything if I die childless, which, right now, is the case. The cigarettes will last much longer than the Dessants did."

They had circled the small plantation, Dr. Gardiner pointing out things like a tour guide. Then they left the plantation for the highway. Louis turned to look out the bus window. "This feels so comfortable. Not like on an airplane, so cold and sterile. I don't like being cold. And I like to know there are people around me."

He quoted a line from a French poem, something she did not recognize. "'Which has killed more people, passion or loneliness?'"

"I don't know that quote," she said.

"Modern. I read it somewhere, I don't remember, but it stuck with me."

No wonder, she thought.

"I think we have one more plantation to visit. Then we will go back to campus."

"Maybe you want to stay awake," said Bishou. "We're going up into the mountains."

"These are the Appalachian Mountains, *n'est-ce pas?*"

"That's correct."

"Where are the Smokies?"

"Great Smoky Mountains? You're looking at them. The Appalachians have a different name in each state."

"What are they called, in your region?"

"White Mountains in New Hampshire, Berkshires in Massachusetts, Green Mountains in Vermont. I've seen them all, at one time or another."

"Ah, you said. Hiking." He pronounced it as the French had adopted it, hi-KING. "Do you miss the mountains?"

"Not really. Being with my family was more important."

"I understand." Louis smiled.

They visited one more tobacco plantation. Now that Bishou knew what Louis was thinking, she could see his focus on cotton and the filters. However, it was definitely a two-way communication, because the hosts and Louis's fellow travelers wanted to know just as much about the tobacco business on his island.

By the time they got back to the university campus, darkness had fallen. As they left the bus, Louis asked, "You teach tomorrow morning, do you not?"

"Oh, yes. I should have reminded you. You're on your own for the first session."

"*D'accord.* Now I will know to expect it. I will see you for the second?" he inquired.

"Yes, I'll see you then."

"*D'accord.* I am going out for dinner with the others, and will see you in the morning. *Bonne nuit.*"

"*Bonne nuit.*"

All the riders had faded into the distance before she heard someone call her name. "Miss Howard?" The bus driver walked toward her, carrying a white jacket.

"Oh, no," she said. "Is that Mr. Dessant's jacket?"

"Yes, Ma'am. He forgot it. Can you give it to him tomorrow?"

"Sure," she said, but her hands were already loaded with her purse and tote bag.

"Wait," said the driver with a grin. He wrapped it around her shoulders. "There you go."

"Thanks. If he should ask for it, tell him I've got it."

"Yes, Ma'am. Goodnight."

"Goodnight."

Back at her apartment, she draped the jacket over an easy chair. The off-white jacket was as clean and neat as Louis was, smelling a little of cologne, a little of tobacco smoke. In dismay, she realized that the only way she could carry it around tomorrow was the same way she did tonight, by wearing it, because she would have the same load in her arms.

Chapter 5

Louis Dessant had on a fresh shirt, no jacket, and was taking his coffee break sitting with some of the other men on the wall of a planter in front of the Conference Center. Louis stood and smiled as Bishou hurried over to them.

"Sorry," she panted, setting down her bag. "By the way, I've got your jacket at my apartment."

"Ah." Louis continued to stand after the other men sat down again. "You will sit, also, and I will bring you coffee. Fair is fair."

"Oh, no, thanks. I can—"

One eyebrow raised, a warning hand came up. "*Asseyez-vous*, Mademoiselle."

"*Oui*, Monsieur." She sat down.

He went to get her coffee.

Gray Jackson chuckled. "He's a gentleman, all the way through."

She nodded. "It's very disconcerting. I'm used to dealing with college students."

All the men laughed.

Vig said, "I never thought about us spoiling you, Missy, but I guess we are."

"You are. It will be dreadfully difficult, going back to teaching undergraduates."

"I'm gonna say what Louis says, that I'm glad I came to this conference," Vig said. "I've learned a lot, not only about tobacco and research, but about colleges. Now I know how to get in contact with the researchers, and I've talked to a lot of the new blood. Some of 'em have some good ideas—even tobacco farmers from other countries, like Louis. Y'know, he takes it all the way from the seed to the carton. A lot of 'em don't, and don't know how."

There was a mutter of general agreement.

"For me," said Bishou, "it was more about the university. I knew EVU runs on tobacco money, but I never really knew what that involved. Now I do."

"There should be a required film about that," said Gray. "You hear so much about student riots and all, and they're biting the hands that feed them."

Bishou shook her head. "It's like having your own teenager in the house, except there are a couple thousand of them. You never know which way the cat is going to jump. You just have to keep your eyes open for a chance to teach them something they're willing to listen to."

"Spoken by the girl with three brothers." Gray toasted her with his coffee, and winked.

"Well, that's true." Bishou looked up as Louis reappeared, with croissants and two coffees on a tiny tray. "Where did you lift the tray? I expected you'd have them in a napkin."

"I asked the cafeteria ladies. They gave me a tray."

"Cafeteria ladies don't give anything to anyone," she said suspiciously.

"I was humble," he replied, looking up with a deerlike expression in his brown eyes.

Again, the men laughed. Gray said, "You just blindside all the ladies with that French sex appeal, Dessant."

"I won't pretend I don't know what that means," said Louis. He sat and put the tray between himself and Bishou, and then broke up a croissant. "But I don't think I have it, or my life would have been much easier."

One of the cafeteria ladies came around with a box for their garbage. She gathered up the little tray, too, with a smile at Louis. The men went back inside, grumbling about the forthcoming lecture, sounding like elderly college students. "Can't make me worried about what I don't know yet," Vig rumbled, and Louis glanced at Bishou in amusement.

However, the Future of the Tobacco Industry included filter cigarettes, and got their full attention., After the session ended, they broke for lunch. The wives joined their husbands.

As they started to cross the campus, Bishou told Louis, "Save me a place. I'll go get your jacket."

Sukey said, "Why don't you go with her, Louis, and get your own jacket?" She was rewarded with suspicious stares from both Louis and Bishou, which she ignored. "We'll save your places. Git."

As they walked toward Bishou's apartment, Louis said, "Madame Hanson has her ideas."

"She certainly does, doesn't she?" Bishou agreed. "Why didn't you argue her out of them?"

"She is one of those women to whom it is easier to say '*oui, Madame*,' and just do it. I noticed you did not argue with her either."

"I think you're right," said Bishou. "As much as I like her. She's definitely 'my way or the highway.' "

He chuckled. "I had not heard that rhyme before, but I understand it completely."

As they walked up the path to Garrison Apartments, Dessant observed, "This is not a dormitory, is it?"

"No. These are apartments for graduate students. My assistantship pays for over half of my expenses here, including this—a very good deal. In some places, one only gets half-tuition, and must pay almost double rates for everything else."

"That's not fair."

"Graduate students are in no position to argue." She pulled out her keys, unlocked the big glass front door, and ushered him inside.

Marie Norton was in the lobby, with the mailroom door open, sorting mail. "Hi, Bishou." She looked carefully at the guest. "I'm Mrs. Norton, resident here."

It was a hint for an introduction. Bishou obliged. "Marie, this is Louis Dessant, from the World Tobacco Conference. Monsieur Dessant, Madame Norton, our manager."

"How do you do, Madame," said Louis politely.

"Oh, my," said Marie. "As in Dessant Cigarettes?" She laughed at their stares. "I did my junior year abroad, Bishou, don't you remember?"

Bishou laughed. "I totally forgot. Yes, as in Dessant Cigarettes."

Louis smiled, too. "My name precedes me."

"Is this your first trip to America?"

"Yes, it is."

"Well, welcome. What brings you to Garrison today?"

"The bus driver from yesterday gave me Mr. Dessant's jacket to return to him, and I ran out of hands this morning," Bishou explained. "I said I'd return it during the lunch break."

The resident apartment door was open, and they heard a baby begin to cry. "Well, it was nice to meet you, Mr. Dessant," said Marie Norton with a smile. "Welcome to EVU. Anything we can do to help, let us know."

"Thank you," Louis replied and followed Bishou up the dark, carpeted stairs. In the stairwell, he murmured very quietly, in French, "I don't have to leave fingerprints, do I?"

Bishou chuckled. "No, but she is good security."

"I trust your word on that. She is young, for this job. I heard a baby."

"*Oui*. Her husband is training at the law school. He studies, and she provides them a place to live while they start their family."

"Whew. That is a grand commitment, much to do at once."

"Certainly it is," said Bishou. "I have true respect for her."

Bishou unlocked her apartment door and ushered Louis inside. He stood and looked around him—the first time she could recall seeing him move his head as well as his eyes—at the bulging bookshelves, the tatty couch, the desk and typewriter.

"So this is your nest? I should perhaps not come in further, *hein*?" He saw his jacket, hung over the back of her desk chair, and lifted it. "What is this?"

She looked, too. "Uh, oh. Did I get lipstick on your collar?"

"It looks red," he agreed.

"Oh, I'm sorry. I'll get some lighter fluid from my bedroom. Wait here."

She stepped into her bedroom and opened a few drawers, searching for the lighter fluid. She found the bottle and started back toward the living room, just in time to hear Louis speak.

"*Oh, mon Dieu*," he groaned, then collapsed on the floor with a thud.

***

Bishou stood paralyzed for a moment. Then she ran to the door, opened it, and shouted, "Marie! *Marie!*"

Then she knelt beside Louis and gripped his shoulder. "Monsieur Dessant. Louis! Wake up. *Levez-vous!*"

Marie was at the door in record time. "Bishou, What happened?"

"I don't know!" She looked up at Marie with wild eyes. "I stepped away to clean a spot off his jacket, and while I was out of the room he just fainted."

"Let's get him up on the couch," said Marie.

Bishou took hold of his shoulders and Marie grabbed his feet. Manhandling was something she could do. Between them, the women got him up onto the couch. Marie slipped off his shoes while Bishou undid his tie and collar. He was still unresponsive.

"Oh God, oh God," said Bishou, "I just expected to hand him his jacket, and leave."

"I'm going downstairs to call Emergency Services," said Marie, who had the only telephone in the building other than a pay phone. "Last thing we need is for one of the conference attendees to have a heart attack here."

"Heart attack?" Bishou gasped.

"You stay with him, honey, while I call the doc."

"Wait a minute, wait a minute." Bishou scribbled on a paper on her desk. "Here's a name—Gray Jackson, he's one of the coordinators for the World Tobacco Conference. He was meeting us at lunch. Call the Barrington dining rooms and tell Gray what's happened."

"I'll do that," she agreed. "We don't need university trouble."

"Amen," said Bishou anxiously. She was glad that Marie left the door open for Emergency Services to find them when she went downstairs This was a university emergency, all right. She sat on a wooden chair close to the couch, the one on which she had hung Louis's jacket, and clasped his hand. It was ice cold.

What made her glance at her desk, she did not know. She saw the papers, half out of the express envelope, and suddenly realized what happened. He had been standing there, waiting for her to get the lighter fluid. He saw an envelope on her desk, papers sticking out the end. The words printed on it were French. Out of curiosity, he pulled the papers out—and saw his own portrait and that damned article. She'd only gone weak-kneed when she saw them. He had fainted.

She rose and put the papers back in the envelope. Then she tucked it into the busiest bookcase, where no one would find it unless undertaking a serious search for it.

"This is my fault," she whispered to herself.

She sat down again on the chair and heard footsteps running up the stairs. Two college EMTs dashed into the room.

"Miss Howard? I'm Jimmy Falcon," said one of them. "This our patient?"

"Yes." She stood up so the EMT could have the chair.

"Can you tell me anything about him, Miss Howard, other than that he's attending the Tobacco Conference?" The man took Dessant's pulse. His partner made notes on a clipboard.

"I can't tell you much. I'm just an interpreter. We walked across campus to pick up his jacket. He left it on the bus yesterday and they gave to me to return to him. His name is Louis Dessant, L-O-U-I-S D-E-S-S-A-N-T, from Réunion Island, a French-owned island off the coast of Africa. He runs a tobacco plantation there." They didn't say Dessant as in the cigarettes, so she did not feel obliged to tell them. "There was a stain on the jacket, and while I was getting my spot cleaner from the bedroom, I heard the thud of him hitting the floor."

The second EMT wrote this down, while the first took Louis's blood pressure.

"Do you know his age?" asked the second EMT.

"I happen to. Thirty-five."

"Smoke, drink?"

"He's a tobacco man. What do you think?" she answered, and both EMTs chuckled.

"So he doesn't have a local doctor, then, does he?" asked Jimmy.

"No, and I don't think student insurance will cover him," she replied.

"We'll take that up with the Tobacco Conference," said the second EMT. "It's their problem, not yours, Miss Howard."

"Still. These are all nice guys," she replied. "I've enjoyed working with them. I worry about them."

The EMT listened to Louis's heart, lifted his eyelids, checked his ears, and then his eyes and mouth with the light. Then Jimmy said, "I'm not 100 percent sure on this, but my first guess would be plain old exhaustion. He's been overdoin' it, flying halfway around the world and goin' to all these conference sessions."

"That seems pretty likely," said Bishou, "but Marie Norton wanted to make sure it wasn't a heart attack."

"It wasn't. He'll come around soon. Before he does, though, we're gonna take some blood for tests, just to make sure." Jimmy suited actions to words, sliding up Louis's sleeve and banding his arm tightly. He drew blood into a hypodermic and transferred it to other vials. "We'll probably be back in touch, if not with you, then with Mr. Dessant himself. But I think he's gonna be fine."

"Thank you," she said, relieved.

"He should rest where he is until tomorrow."

"Huh?" Bishou stared at the EMT. "I'm a female grad student, and this is my apartment he's in."

Jimmy reddened. "I know it might look bad, but it'd look even worse if he fell and broke his leg or arm or neck, Miss Howard. And I don't think you'd want to pay for the ambulance to haul him up and down these stairs. He can go home tomorrow if a friend drives him over. Otherwise—you've got yourself a house guest."

"The university will have fits," she muttered.

"I'll send them a copy of the emergency report, too," the EMT replied. "He's to take it easy for twenty-four hours, and then he can be transported back to his hotel room if someone gives him a ride."

They gathered up their materials and equipment, and left. Almost immediately, Marie Norton was in the door. "What did they say?"

"Not a heart attack," said Bishou, and saw Marie slump in relief. "They say it's just jet lag and exhaustion. But they don't want him moved until tomorrow."

"*Pas de probleme*," quipped Marie, adding dryly. "No one can ever accuse you of sneaking a man up to your room, Bishou. You do it with fanfare."

"I guess that's true, but I'm going to take an awful lot of heat for this."

"I know better," said Marie, "and I'm on your side. Dean Chambers or anyone wants to complain, bring 'em on."

"Thanks so much, Marie," Bishou sighed.

"He is attractive, though," Marie mused, "and I'm a judge." Considering Marie's head-resident stories, this was probably true.

"I know. But it's no secret he's a widower and still carrying the torch for his first wife. I'm safe as safe can be."

"Unless he starts walking in his sleep."

"My brother the Sergeant Major has taught me some self-defense tricks. I'm *still* safe as safe can be."

The front doorbell sounded. Marie left to answer it, saying, "Back to work. Keep the faith, Bishou."

"Right."

She sat down again on the chair near Louis. She heard creaking stairs and the sounds of whispers and murmurs in the hallway, so she was ready for the tobacco people when they appeared in the doorway.

Gray Jackson grinned and asked, "We got the right apartment, Lady?"

Bishou smiled and motioned them in.

Sukey Hansen took the easy chair, and looked very chastened. "I'm sorry, honey. I didn't expect this to happen when I sent you both over for his coat."

"Yeah," said Gray, "she expected maybe a little nooky in the hallway."

"Shut up, Gray Jackson," said Sukey.

"What the hell happened?" asked Vig.

"The EMTs say he's just been overdoing it," Bishou replied. "Between the jet lag and all the socializing he's been doing with you guys, he just fainted. It's exhaustion, nothing more." Saying more felt unnecessary, too.

"How's he getting back to the hotel?" asked Gray.

"I'm not even going to worry about that until he's conscious," Bishou replied.

"I'm gonna stay here with you, honey," Sukey said quietly. "At least for a while."

"Thanks, Sukey," Bishou said, equally quietly. "I appreciate the support."

"My pleasure, honey." She looked up at her husband and Gray. "You know, Bishou never did get any lunch. Why don't you boys go over and pick up a box lunch for her, and something for us to drink?"

"That's a plan," said Vig, as the men left.

Bishou rubbed her eyes. Then she realized Sukey was looking at her, very thoughtfully.

"Want to tell me what happened?" Sukey asked, in that same quiet tone.

It was a strong temptation. "Not yet."

"All right. Then later."

Louis groaned.

They both turned to look at him.

"Carola."

Sukey looked at Bishou. "Carola?"

"His wife," Bishou said.

Louis spoke again. A second time, a third time. Bishou felt sick to her stomach.

"What did he say?" Sukey prodded.

"He said, 'I know what you are doing. Don't you think I know you are poisoning me? Fill it up! I love you more than anything. I don't want to live without you.'" Bishou took a deep breath as he spoke a fourth time, then translated. "He said, 'Kill me. I would rather die than leave your side.'"

He repeated, "Carola. Carola."

Bishou got a handkerchief and wiped tears from his face. Once again, Louis fell silent.

Bishou stood, went to her tiny bathroom, got a washcloth, and dampened it. She knelt beside the couch, and wiped his face with it.

"*Merci,*" he said, either in his dreams or not.

"*De rien,*" she replied quietly.

"*Si froid.*"

"'So cold.'" She turned to Sukey. "Could you get one of the blankets off my bed?"

Sukey nodded. In a moment, she returned with a coverlet, which the two women wrapped snugly around him. They returned to their seats.

"So tell me about him," said Sukey.

"I'd rather not." Bishou rubbed her eyes. "It's not my secret to tell, really."

"But you stumbled across one of Louis's secrets?"

Bishou nodded. "An item in my research for my doctoral dissertation. And he saw it on my desk."

"Lordy. And he fainted. It didn't mean to you what it did to him."

"That's it," said Bishou, in lieu of a lie. But it was no lie when she added, "I feel so bad. I wish he'd never seen it. I never thought about him coming here to get his jacket."

"Don't beat yourself up," said Sukey. "It's my fault, too. I should never have suggested it, but how was I to know?"

They lapsed into silence, watching the sleeping patient. The room was very quiet for a long time. Bishou saw Louis's hands and feet twitch, then his face. *He should be waking up soon*, she thought. Then, suddenly, he sat up, screaming.

Sukey jumped back, but Bishou dived for Louis. She grabbed one of his wrists and put an arm around his shoulders. He fought her. "Ssh, ssh," she urged. "*Doucement, doucement.*" Gently, gently.

"*Oh, mon Dieu,*" he sobbed. "*Ou est-il?*"

"I have hidden it," she replied in French. "No one knows."

"Oh, non, non," he cried. "Where did you find that horrible thing? I hoped never to see it again!"

"It came from Paris in my university research for my doctoral degree. I am so sorry, Louis. Please forgive me."

"Oh mon Dieu, mon Dieu. I fainted." He saw Sukey. "And all the world knows it."

"*Non*, the world knows nothing," she said, still speaking French. "The doctors came here and said that you fainted from exhaustion and *décalage*. They did not see the paper, either. They did not know why you collapsed. Only you and I know what you saw."

"Bishou," he wept, "what have you done to me?"

"I am sorry. Please, Louis, there are people here now. You must be strong. I will help you. This will pass." She kept her voice strong, but quiet, and she held him just as Bat held Marine meltdowns that still appeared on his doorstep from time to time. And this was a meltdown, for certain.

Louis took a deep breath. Bishou wiped his face with the cool, damp cloth. Slowly, it occurred to him that Bishou was holding him tightly, and hadn't let go. In English, he said, "Mademoiselle, if you do not release me, Madame will think there is more to our relationship than the truth."

Bishou smiled, and sat back, relieved. Sukey looked as relieved as she did. "My Lord, Louis, you gave us a fright. I'm going to send you to bed like one of my teenage boys, from now on."

"Not for a night or so," said Bishou. "Tonight he's staying here, on the couch."

"*Quoi?*" Louis asked, startled.

"Doctor's orders." Bishou's mouth tightened. "They said you're too weak to walk very far, so they don't want you walking anywhere, nor climbing stairs. Here you stay. Tomorrow, the Hansens can pick you up and take you to the hotel."

"No," he said firmly. "I am here for the conference. This is—" He said a phrase in French.

"Just a minor setback. I know, and you may be right. But the only thing the university is more worried about than propriety is injury. If you hurt yourself, it would be even worse for the conference."

Louis made a face. Before he could say anything, a voice called out from the door, "We're back! We brought take-out chicken instead. That okay with everyone?" Vig and Gray entered carrying bags and boxes.

"Heeey, Louis!" Gray reached out to shake his hand. "Welcome back."

"I am glad to be here. What is it that smells so good? *Poulet*?"

"Yes, chicken," Bishou answered. "But go easy. You've had a rough day."

Louis growled. He pulled himself upright on the couch, the blanket still wrapped around his legs. Vig, Gray, and Sukey invaded Bishou's pathetic little kitchenette.

"Cryin' out loud, Bishou," called Gray. "Don't you even have three glasses that match?"

"Why do I need three glasses? I wash out the one I use as soon as I use it," she called back.

Louis chuckled. She started to rise, but he grabbed her hands and pulled her onto the couch beside him.

"Stay here," he advised. "Let them learn about graduate student apartments by themselves."

"I suppose you're right."

He put his arm around her shoulder. "Things like this, I am always right."

"I am very sorry to shock you," she said.

"We will talk later, when everyone has gone."

"Hey! Chardonnay!"

"Go easy on that stuff," she called. "That's what I feed my boss."

"Did I hear my name?" Dr. Roth stood at the door.

"Aiiee," said Bishou, very quietly, and stood up.

Sukey, however, beat her to the punch. "We're gonna owe you a whole case of Chardonnay for lending us Bishou Howard," she said with a smile, taking Roth's hand and pulling him into the tiny living room.

"I came over to see if Bishou's day was as rough as I'd heard it was."

"Uh-oh," said Bishou. "Marie Norton, or the dean?"

"Both, actually." Roth held out a hand to Louis. "Monsieur

Dessant, so nice to meet you. I'm Dr. Raymond Roth, of the literature department."

"Ah. Mademoiselle's advisor?"

They shook hands, and Roth slid into his favorite chair. Bishou sat down again on her wooden desk chair.

"Yes, that's correct. The university wanted me to check up on you, too, and make sure you were all right, because—after a fashion—you are one of Miss Howard's students."

"Indeed, I am." That businesslike French accent never sounded nicer. "I am grateful for all her help, and I am most apologetic for being such a burden to the school."

Roth made himself comfortable in the chair. "Well, it's taught us one thing, at least, that we shouldn't hit the ground running with overseas students. We need to give them a day or two to adjust to the strain of airline travel."

"I think that might be necessary," Louis admitted. "I am sure that is what happened to me, exhaustion and *décalage*—jet lag."

"I can't help feeling we've met before," said Roth.

Louis chuckled. "We have. You were in the back of the lecture hall the day I stopped in to see the college class. I have never attended university. I was curious. We spoke a few words."

"Not enough for me to realize your native language was French," said Roth, grimacing. "My apologies."

"*De rien.*" Louis smiled, and got more comfortable on the couch. "I am glad to know for certain who you are, because I knew Mademoiselle Howard respected Dr. Roth greatly. Please do not—what is the word?—penalize her for my foolishness."

"No, no, of course not. What happened here was so obviously an accident—and it is well documented by the head resident and by medical reports." Roth stood. "Well, I just came by to see how everything was. Now I'll move on. I promised my wife I'd be home by dinnertime. Goodbye, Bishou. I'll see you on Friday."

Bishou sighed. "I am in *so* much trouble."

"How so?" asked Louis in surprise.

"They told me not to get personal about this job, and here I've got a whole bunch of you partying in my apartment," she said unhappily.

"Maybe you're being a bit straitlaced Yankee about this," Sukey suggested.

"Yeah, well, maybe you don't know academia. It's worse than a small town. Gossip travels at the speed of sound, and they're quite willing to believe the worst on no evidence at all."

Louis, his hand resting against his cheek, smiled and said, "Maybe you should just have some chicken and deal with one problem at a time." Then he struggled to raise himself from the couch—and slid to a pile on the floor. He growled something ugly and explosive.

"Okay if I don't translate that one?" Bishou asked him, as the men helped lift him.

He growled again. Gray helped him navigate to the bathroom, and he came back to the couch by himself.

The chicken, mashed potatoes, baked beans, and coleslaw may not have been great art, but they filled the gap, washed down by iced tea and the last of the Chardonnay.

"I dunno, Louis," Gray teased with a grin, as they got up to return to the afternoon sessions. "Leaving you here, helpless, at a woman's mercy . . ."

Louis smiled up at him. "I think I am safe here, *mon ami*. Tomorrow morning, however, can someone pick me up at seven in the morning? I must go back to my room, shave, and change clothes."

"Sure, I'll arrange it," Gray confirmed.

Sukey said, "We'll be back this evening to see if you kids need anything."

"All right," said Bishou. "Thank you." She showed her guests to the door, and closed it at last.

Louis stretched out again on the couch and wrapped the blanket around him. "How were you planning to spend the rest of your day? If you must leave me here alone, I promise I will not rob you."

"No, I was planning to work on my dissertation. That's why I had the papers out. Will the typing bother you?"

"No. What have you got to read in French?"

Bishou scooped a handful of paperbacks out of the bookshelf and piled them on the floor beside him. Louis went carefully through the pile, finally selecting a tired paperback. "Ah! I haven't seen one of these since I was a child. Was this adventure story Bat's or yours?"

"We both like them," Bishou smiled, and sat at her desk to work. Soon, she was involved in the argument of her thesis, and he was quietly reading on the couch.

Bishou worked for well over an hour, satisfied that her notes were shaping up. Then she rolled three sheets of paper with carbon papers sandwiched between them into her typewriter to type a couple more precious pages in triplicate. She glanced at Louis, absorbed in the adventure story, a little smile on his lips. *He really is easy to please*, she thought.

She got up to find a reference or two, brought the books back to her desk, sat down, wrote a little more, and then typed more. It was slow going, but solid work—what a dissertation needed.

Bishou glanced at Louis again. She was surprised to find he was lying on his side, without a book, watching her. He closed his eyes quickly, as if he'd been caught out.

"*Quoi?*" Then she glanced down at herself. She hadn't adjusted her clothing when she sat down again in the chair, and her skirt had shimmied up. She showed quite an expanse of leg and garter. Bishou snorted, and pulled down the skirt. "Monsieur Dessant."

Louis opened his eyes, that same smile on his lips. "Well, I am a man. I could not help but look."

She felt her face burn. His smile vanished.

In a different tone, he said, "While there is no one else around, let us discuss those papers."

"All right."

"Are you planning to document me in your thesis?"

"No," she replied, honestly.

"Then why do you have those clippings? Why should my name be in some university binder forever?"

"It won't be there, I swear it, Louis."

"Then why have them? Why save those horrible things?" he insisted.

"I have them because the author refers to various books on the subject, and then draws references from life. I don't draw references from life in my dissertation, not at all."

"Pfah!" He turned his head in disbelief.

Bishou understood, and it made her smile. "Let me explain about degree candidacy, Monsieur. A candidate for an advanced degree goes before an examination panel. The members of this panel may be drawn from anywhere in the world, depending on the subject matter. So—the material referred to in the dissertation must be equally available to all of them. That means not a television show, not a clipping, not an oral history, but printed matter. Mainly, books. Nothing may be involved that the professor from Guelph cannot research as easily as the professor from Lyon."

"They are from all over the world, these inquisitors?"

She nodded. "I have no idea who they will be yet. They may not even tell me. But Dr. Roth will arrange for them all to be in a certain place at a certain time, to ask me questions so I can defend my thesis. They accept or deny my application for an advanced degree, and I either receive the degree or I start again."

"And what do you get out of all this?" he asked intently.

"The title of Doctor Bishou Howard, and three stripes on my gown," Bishou replied with a smile. "Pretty silly, isn't it?"

"A man who is learning how to stuff cotton in the ends of cigarettes is not going to tell you three stripes on a gown are silly."

"Thank you for taking such a fair view of it. You've spoken very decently to me during this entire conference, and I appreciate it. I know the others don't mean anything by their comments, but sometimes, they make it difficult for me."

"You have a dream and a purpose," he said. "Do not lose either one. I know how—desolated—one can become, if one loses the dream. I had dreams once. At least I still have a purpose."

"What do you mean?" she asked.

"My dreams—to marry, have a family, have a good life." Louis stared toward the opposite wall introspectively. "That is all gone now, dust. But the purpose? Dessant Cigarettes, it keeps me going. To make a business that Etien can run when I am gone, and that will give a good life to his children after him." He smiled at her, but the smile was sad. "That newspaper cannot tell it all. It cannot tell you what a good man Etien Campard is, how he saw the beginnings of my downfall, but knew I wouldn't listen, how he tried to prevent my ruin. Nor how he gave me refuge and money when I was a criminal, and stood by me after my arrest. The newspaper cannot tell you all that Etien did to save me from my own passions, and failed. He pressed for my release from prison. He has always been my best friend. I owe him so much."

"The newspaper never even mentions Etien," she said.

"I am glad. It keeps him safe from the harpies. I tell you the truth, Bishou—I know whenever there is another article about Carola and me, because I get scores of letters from women who want to rehabilitate me. I will be a marked man all my life, the fallen one."

"Mmm-hmm." Bishou folded her arms. "I could show you the letters from men telling me to give up my foolishness about getting a PhD in literature, a real woman doesn't need that."

Again, that sad smile. "I suppose it is similar—give up the

dream, it isn't manly. Or maidenly. I am glad that you do not give up on your dreams, Bishou. Mine are gone. Etien says no, I must still dream, and I dare not tell him differently because he has been always right and I have been always wrong."

"You loved Carola very much, Louis. That was real."

One more sad smile. He reached into his pants pocket, pulled out a wallet, and handed a photograph to Bishou. An incredibly beautiful green-eyed woman wore a bridal veil over her blond hair and looked not quite at the camera, as if she didn't really want her image captured forever.

Bishou took a very long look, then handed it back. "She's beautiful, Louis."

"Yes, she was. I lost my heart to her the first moment I saw her. Now Etien does not permit me to mention her name, and I must keep the photograph to myself. But this portrait has done its duty. When I showed it to the judges, they found extenuating circumstances for my crimes."

Louis put the photo back in his wallet and slid the wallet back in his pocket. Then he lay down on the couch. Bishou realized that his mind was far from here.

She returned to her deskwork. For a long time, she just stared into space. Then, Bishou got a piece of paper, and started to write.

Chapter 6

It was a long letter for a telegram, and was written in French. At the top were the date and the address: 7 Rue Calaincourt, F-1215 St. Denis, Ile de la Réunion. CONFIDENTIEL.

> *Cher M. Howard,*
>
> *I am glad to receive your letter. I had a brief message from Louis, from Washington, saying he was on his way and the flight had been good. I suspect that you are correct, it is décalage and strain of the trip to America that have caused his collapse. I had not expected to hear from him, but I was worried about his health. As you have guessed, this is not the first time he has fallen from nervous exhaustion.*
>
> *Also as you have guessed, yes, he is the notorious Louis Dessant. I think and hope most of that bad publicity has died down. What you said in your transmission makes me think, as well, that no one remembers it. That is a good thing and a great relief to me, for he is one of the best men I have ever known.*
>
> *As his own physician would attest, Louis pushes himself to exhaustion, and then has nerve-storms. Sometimes, as I suspect happened here, it is triggered off by some event—no doubt, as you said, seeing that damnable Paris Gazette article. In a perfect world, I wish I could say that a rest cure will rehabilitate him—but as you may also know, it was during his rest cure in Lyons that he discovered the location of the woman who betrayed him, and met her again!*
>
> *That was the beginning of the end for him, for she ensnared him once more and he murdered another man for her sake, sold his half of our business to me, lost the money, and went on the run with her. It ended badly, but how else could it have ended? Louis took his punishment like a man, and there were*

many besides myself who pushed for his release. The blame was solely Carola's—I will never call her Mme. Dessant, although Louis does—and may her sins rest on her head for all eternity. She befouled a good man, in my opinion, although Louis does not see it that way at all. He loved her passionately.

Louis is a fine man. Make no mistake in that. I am a coward by comparison. He is the brave entrepreneur, with new ideas, pushing to make the business work. I am the housewife who stays behind to mind the store. I am a family man, not a businessman. Buying him out, and running the entire business myself, was my idea of hell. I was very glad that the Sûreté recovered his sales money as evidence, and I was eventually able to reclaim it and press him to take back his half of our business. Such a relief for me!

I hope that, out of sight of his friends and neighbors of the island, he can work his way through his troubles and come back to us. I was hoping he would come back refreshed, but perhaps that is too much to hope. Perhaps, as you suggested in your transmission, I did see symptoms of something and hoped that a change of venue would make a difference to him. I hadn't expected this, I promise you.

The physician says, a mild tranquilizer to help him sleep, or a simple headache pill, is all he should need. (Dr. Ferenc is also our family physician.) Louis doesn't take many drugs, and not even more than a drink or two in the evenings. Cool compresses if he wants them, perhaps a neck massage if you have a masseur available, but it is not necessary. The best thing for him, Ferenc says, is to get him home and back into his old routine. But first we must get him here. There's no other man I would be afraid of losing on two straight airplane trips, Washington to Paris and Paris to Saint-Denis, except him. I will not relax until I see him crossing the tarmac at Garros. Please do everything you can to make sure he is on that first leg of the flight, short of bolting him to the seat! I may come to Paris myself, to make sure he is on the second leg.

I know I have asked you to keep this letter confidential, but please, tell him Dr. Ferenc's instructions and tell him I will be looking for him at Orly.

Thank you for your help in this matter.

Sincerely, Etien Campard

***

The tobacco crowd, an enlarged group of North Carolinians and curious Texans, came to Bishou's apartment that evening with pizza (or as they called it, pizza pie), chips, and "pop." Louis had never had pizza before, so they had great fun with him. He was obviously getting his strength back, barely touching furniture in passing as he made his way to the bathroom or the kitchen. They would not allow him to pitch in and dry dishes, however; Sukey sent him back to the couch with the menfolk around him, while the women—Bishou, Sukey, Isabel, and Sondra—stayed in the kitchen.

"How'd you spend your afternoon?" Sukey asked Bishou.

"I worked on my dissertation, and Louis read old French paperbacks that I had kicking around," Bishou replied.

"I see at least he's 'Louis' now," Sukey observed.

"Tomorrow morning he'll be Monsieur Dessant again, and I'll be Mademoiselle Howard. But he did spend the afternoon camped on my couch."

"His color looks better," Sukey agreed.

Bishou nodded. "It does. Maybe an afternoon lying on a couch, reading trashy French novels, was just what he needed."

"You nervous about having him here for the night?"

"A little. Then I think of having three brothers camped out in my dorm room half this size, and realize this is the height of luxury by comparison."

"I suppose that's true," Isabel chuckled.

"But man, Bishou, you lucked out," said Sondra. "The hot, unmarried one is the one who passes out on your couch. I am envious, girl, reputation or not."

"You're all married," grinned Bishou. "You can talk."

"Don't you think he's cute?" Sondra asked.

"Sure he is," Bishou defended herself, "but I'm bespoke. By East Virginia University."

"EVU will be done by the end of the year," Sondra predicted. "If I were you, I'd keep that guy's number in my little black book."

"What're you going to do after you graduate from here?" Isabel asked.

"Get a job. But to teach at the college level, I need that degree first."

"Any idea where yet?"

"Not a clue. When I get set up, I've got to help my brother, Bat, take care of our younger brothers. Our parents are pretty much too old and helpless to do it."

"Then are you gonna get married?" asked Sondra.

"I don't know when or if I'm going to be able to fit that in," Bishou admitted, "if I find the right man."

"The right man's on that couch," said Sondra. "Don't lose that number."

Chapter 7

Morning came. Bishou had slept soundly. She'd heard Louis moving around during the night, from the couch to the bathroom, and once she thought the kitchen light came on. When her alarm chimed, she shut it off, tottered into the bathroom to wash up, and then back into the bedroom to change her clothes. Then she went into her tiny living room-study.

Louis's beard had grown during the night, and of course he had slept in his clothes. He looked tatty, but no worse than her brother would have. He yawned and stretched. "Mmm—time to get up?"

"Yes. It's six-thirty. I can make some coffee, if you wish."

"No, thank you. I will wait until I wash and change at the hotel. The *médecin* was right. I feel much stronger now."

He didn't look it.

Bishou wrung out a washcloth, and brought it out to Louis, who still lay, tired and dispirited, on the couch. She sat down on the wooden chair and leaned toward him.

"Did you sleep well?" she asked him, in French.

"I did not sleep much," he admitted. Even his voice was tired. "I am hot, and I feel very foolish."

"Don't feel that way." She took the washcloth from him and folded it. "Here, let me put this cool compress on your forehead. It will help."

Louis closed his eyes and leaned back again. He let her press the damp cloth in place. "Mmm. Feels good."

Bishou rose and got aspirin and a tumbler of water from her tiny bathroom. "And one aspirin should be all you need." Bishou placed the aspirin in his hand. Louis opened his eyes and took it, swallowing it with difficulty. He took a drink of water to help it down.

"I don't take much medicine," he said, "so a little should do much."

Bishou smiled. "That's what Dr. Ferenc said."

His eyes opened suddenly and he sat up. "Ferenc? *My* Doctor Ferenc?"

"Will you lie down?"

"I will not. How did you contact him? You don't even have a telephone here."

"That's the advantage of being a researcher. I used the library teletype services to send a message to Dessant Industries. The library thought it was research because it was in French, and didn't charge me for it. Then they got a French answer, again a mystery to them, from a man named Etien Campard."

"My partner!" Louis seemed surprised, but he was also delighted. "I hope you didn't scare him."

"Oh, *non, non.* I told him you had fainted, and wondered if it were *décalage* and fatigue. He said probably yes, it had happened before, and that you would be all right with mild treatment. Dr. Ferenc said compresses, aspirin, and maybe physical therapy if I knew a masseur. But I don't know one, except my brother, and he's too far away."

"That's all right. The rest will help." The smile remained on his lips and in his eyes. "Etien. I am so sorry to worry him."

"Then promise him, even if he cannot hear you, that you will go straight home after the conference. He's worried enough to meet you at Orly."

Louis admitted shyly, "Actually, I would like him to meet me at Orly. I hate traveling alone."

"Good, because he'll be there. I wasn't supposed to tell you that part, so be sure you act surprised when you see him."

Louis smiled in delight, reached out, and drew Bishou against him. He hugged her. "Thank you, *mon amie.*"

"*De rien.* Now let go, before someone sees us and we get into trouble."

"*Oui,* Mademoiselle." Still smiling, Louis released her. "You are a good friend, Mademoiselle."

"And you are one hell of an education, Monsieur."

He laughed, almost boyishly.

There was a knock at the door. Bishou opened it to find a university staff member there.

"I'm here to pick up Mr. Dessant," he said.

"Ah." Louis stood up—without falling over, this time. "My ride." He made sure he had his wallet, pen, and other things in his pockets, and put on his jacket. "This gentleman will take me back to my hotel room, so I can wash and change. Will I see you at the lecture this morning?"

"Probably not. I must see Dr. Roth today."

"Oh." Louis's face grew serious. "You are still in trouble—a man in your apartment, and what the neighbors will say."

"If you don't say a word, I can probably bare-face them out of this," said Bishou. "Just don't help, *d'accord*?"

Again he laughed. "*D'accord.* I am Monsieur Dessant, of the World Tobacco Conference, nothing more." Louis reached out a hand at the same moment Bishou did, and they shook solemnly. "*Au revoir*, Mademoiselle."

"*Au revoir*, Monsieur."

***

Dr. Roth pulled out his bottom file drawer for use as a footstool, as was his custom. Bishou took the only other chair in his tiny office. The door was shut.

"You must have sweated bullets over this."

"I'll say," Bishou agreed.

"And you're working on a thesis on passion. Good God, Bishou, that man is sex in a white package."

"Something like that."

"I think we've soldiered through it okay." Dr. Roth continued to use the pronoun "we," which was a good sign. "Are you willing to assist him for the next week, or do you need to come up for air?"

"Who else could do it?" Bishou asked reasonably. "And besides, I think we're through the worst."

"What was 'the worst,' exactly?" Roth wanted to know. "Something kicked this off, didn't it?"

"Yes." Bishou grimaced ruefully. "Monsieur Dessant and I have agreed to bury it, but it was my fault, in a way. I got copies of some articles from the *Paris Gazette* about modern passion, which included a picture and story about him. When he glanced at my desk, he saw his face staring up at him. That's why he fainted."

"I don't get it. Modern passion?"

"Louis Dessant did seven years at hard labor for a crime of passion," Bishou explained.

"Oh, shit."

"Yeah, well. That wasn't even the reason I had the article. I had it because its author, Georges Goulard, wrote a book, *Sans Merci*. Heard of it? Published five years ago."

"Yes, I read something. Major prize, wasn't it?"

"Honorable mention, yes. But anyway, there was this feature article about crimes of passion, sitting on my desk—"

"And in comes one of its subjects, to pick up his coat."

"Exactly. As I said to Monsieur Dessant, what an education I've gotten out of this. I bet I've apologized to him at least half a dozen times. I also had to promise him that nothing about him or his case will ever appear in my dissertation."

"That shouldn't cripple you. It's not researchable," Dr. Roth observed.

Bishou nodded. "I explained to him about references and reproducibility. Tough concepts to explain to non-academics, but I think he got it. More along the lines of, I have to be able to pick up the same book in Calgary and follow your argument."

"True enough." Dr. Roth sounded relieved. "Let's us bury it, too."

"Fine by me. It's tough enough that he's, as you put it, sex in a white package."

Dr. Roth smiled and cocked an eye at her. "Makes you sweat, does he?"

"And how. He says every time that article is reprinted anywhere, he gets scads of marriage proposals, offers to rehabilitate him, and worse."

Roth laughed. "Most men dream of being in that situation."

"He doesn't. I can't imagine how he can be so—unspoiled—after all he's been through. No, that's not the right word. But anyway, he's only vaguely aware of it."

"Maybe he *is* aware of it, Bishou."

She shook her head. "I'm pretty sure not. My brother Bat has what Louis Dessant has, but the American version. So I recognize it when I see it, but I'm not sure what it is."

"It's the old S.A.," Roth replied. "Sex Appeal and no mistake. One more week, and it's over, Bishou, and you won't see him again."

Chapter 8

Bat's letter was waiting for her when she picked up her mail on the way to the conference.

Hey, Little Sister,

I'm not shouting. See? No capital letters, no underlines. Anyway, I saw that you had your whole list of reasons not to screw up, laid out there for me. To my great relief, I admit.

You're probably just stunned because your dissertation came to life and punched you in the face. But it could be the glamour of escorting a real-life millionaire, too, which I think he is. Don't let it turn your head. I suspect, after all he's been through, that he's been kicked around enough to be human. That could be a plus.

You know, you really could actually be in love, if he's a nice guy. Is he? Not enough to spike our deal, I hope? Doesn't sound like you're fou d'amour, from what you say in your letter.

If he's just here because he's a tourist, and he's meeting some nice Americans including you, it might not be an issue. Keep your eyes front and your (ahem) in your pocket. Being in love is not bad, if you don't let it take over your judgment. Sometimes good judgment is more necessary than love, because we've all got to survive. Sounds like that's where your boy fell down on the job. But I'll be the first man to say that feeling love, whether you show it or not, is an important part of being human.

Enough lecturing. You know by now I'm talking half to myself when I say stuff like this. You and I have just watched out for the family for so long. But Andy's a high school freshman now. Gerry just started seventh grade. Soon they'll be out in the world, and we'll have the freedom we never had. NOT to be in 'Nam. NOT to be a grad student. Oops, sorry,

I said I wouldn't yell in capitals. Better quit now.
Keep the faith.
Love, Bat

Bishou smiled and folded the letter. His words reinforced her thoughts. Her "hitch" here was almost finished. Then, on to greater things. The World Tobacco Conference would fade to just another interesting event in her life.

At the front door of the Medlin Conference Center, she picked up a badge from Annie and wrote her name on it.

"How's Mr. Dessant?" the elderly secretary asked her.

"You've probably seen him since I have," Bishou replied. "Isn't he inside? No point in me going in, if he isn't."

Annie admitted, "Yes, I saw him go in."

The Twiggy look-alike dealt herself in, and commented, "I heard you had an exciting night."

"If you mean someone fainting and me calling Emergency Services, yes, I suppose that could be called exciting." Bishou recapped the marker and set it back on the table. She gave them a quick smile and hurried inside.

Louis had saved a seat for her. He smiled as she sat down. This lecture's topic was "Tobacco Genetics." She understood some things that she had read about nucleic acids and cell biology, but this was a strain to follow. Louis was growling wordlessly, and as she looked around the lecture hall, she realized everyone else was just as lost. She raised her hand. The scientist, of course, looked past her.

Then a deep voice spoke up from the back—Vig Hansen. "Doctor Hunt, I think you should let the lady professor talk." It did not sound like a mere suggestion.

"Yes, then—Professor?" said Dr. Hunt, half-heartedly.

Very humbly, Bishou said, "Dr. Hunt, I think you're losing your audience. They aren't academics, and they aren't trained in genetics. They're farmers."

"And you have suggestions, of course?" he asked coldly.

"No, sir," she said. "It's your lecture. I'm merely an observer."

A few more men's voices cut in. Beside her, Louis Dessant was grinning. From his seat near the back, Vig Hansen said, "Ten bucks says even Bishou Howard can't explain the difference between a phenotype and a genotype to me and make me give a damn."

There was plenty of laughter.

But Louis Dessant slapped his desk and said, "Deal! I will cover."

Bishou stared at him. "Mr. Dessant, are you nuts? I'm a literature professor." She remembered too late that he said he took risks.

"Do it," he challenged her.

Bishou sighed and stood. She walked up to Dr. Hunt, leaned over, and murmured in his ear, "Crap. I'm really sorry about this. I should've warned you they're getting restless and ugly."

Hunt sensed a kindred spirit at last, and murmured, "What are you going to do?"

"Win the bet or die trying," she murmured in reply, then raised her voice. "All right. Phenotype and genotype. And the World Tobacco Conference donates money to the EVU Scholarship Fund, right?"

They turned to look at Gray Jackson, standing in an aisle, who grinned and said, "Right."

"Okay, here we go. Use your imaginations." Bishou started shaping things in the air, on an imaginary table. "I've got three warming racks here, like you see at banquets. Each one has a heat source underneath, and on top, I've got three pans with water in them. Okay so far?"

Masculine grunts.

"Okay, this first pan has water in it. Underneath is canned heat, and I've got one of those clicker flints to start it. Clack—there's my clicker—the canned heat lights up. After a while, the burning stuff heats up the water. There's my hot water. You don't need to know what went into the doings in order to appreciate the hot water at the end. Are you still with me?"

Grunts and yesses.

"The hot water, though, is the phenotype—the result you see—and that flint was the genotype, the mechanism that got everything started.

"Okay, here's my second pan. Up top, water, same as the first. Underneath, there's a tiny dish with just a drop of water in it. I take a lump of magnesium out of the kerosene I usually store it in to keep it from igniting, and pop it into the drop of water for a major chemical reaction." Dr. Hunt started to smile, too. "So the magnesium acts like a flare, do you see? And it heats up the water in the pan, and the result is—a pan of hot water. You still following me?"

More grunts.

"Here's my third pan of water. Underneath it is a gadget I borrowed from the radiation lab—a mini atomic reactor. I pull the damper rod and let it run, and it heats up. It heats the pan of water—and there's your phenotype, hot water."

Now she could hear talking, and approval, and somebody clapped.

"Wait a minute, wait a minute, we're not finished. Now I want to show you the points Dr. Hunt was making. The fire we used to heat our three pans of water came from three different sources—mechanical, chemical, and radiation. Now, suppose, instead of combinations of flammable ingredients, we have combinations of those genes he's been talking about—a physical combination," she pretended to touch the heat source of her first pan, "where the genes, smaller than a microscope can see, are wrapped around each other in such a way that they produce something different. Not hot water. Flavor. Without bite. The flavor you want in your tobacco."

More grunts. Flavor they understood.

"There's flavor in that pan up there, not hot water. Flavor is your phenotype, in this case. And the right genotype can come from a genetic combination that occurs in three ways." Again, she pointed to her three imaginary burners. "Mechanical, chemical, and radiation. Those genes make you, and they can break you. A mechanical combination can be knocked apart, on the genetic level. A chemical combination can be dissolved, maybe by a chemical like DDT, we don't know, we're still studying. And we know radiation combinations are always a risk. The A-bomb proved that. Any of those combinations get knocked apart, by natural or unnatural forces, and suddenly, your flavor phenotype isn't new leaf, it's old socks."

"Thank you for putting it so clearly, Professor," said Dr. Hunt smoothly, picking up where she left off, and going back to his original lecture. However, from time to time, he referred to Bishou's examples, and his crowd settled down.

Just before the break, as Dr. Hunt wound down his lecture, Bishou became aware that someone stood beside her: Vig Hansen. The catcalls and cheers were remarkable as he handed a $10 bill to Louis Dessant. Louis smiled and tucked it in his jacket pocket. His risk had paid off.

"Thank you," said Bishou Howard, "and the EVU Scholarship Fund thanks you, too."

***

President Lanthier laughed and laughed. Looking at Bishou, seated in the guest chair in his office, he almost choked. "So that's what it was! Do you know, those tobacco-men have donated almost $10,000 today?"

Bishou stared. "Holy cow! I thought they were only talking a thousand or so."

"From the Conference, yes. Three thousand. The rest comes from individuals. A couple of them told me that Miss Howard did the university proud today, and we should be spending more money on women like her." He wiped tears of laughter from his eyes, and said, "Okay, do you want me to eat any of the words I've said to you?"

"No, sir, you've been perfectly right all along, and I'm doing my best to live within the guidelines you set. I just didn't—well, you know, they're tobacco men. They take risks."

"And Mr. Dessant backed you, because you've been so good to him," said the President. "You know, he gave us a private donation, too. Six hundred and fifty dollars, all the money he collected on the bet." He was still chuckling. "You were brave enough to take that dare. You didn't know where it would lead you."

"I'm here."

"Well, that's true." President Lanthier pulled out a handkerchief from his pocket and blew his nose. "Sorry if I scared you, summoning you to my office."

"No, sir, I wasn't scared. I just didn't know *what* was going to happen next."

Lanthier asked her, "Do you know what the trouble was with Dessant's visa?"

"No, sir," she replied.

He understood at once. "Is there anything I should know?"

"No, sir."

"Will it affect the conference in any way?"

"No, sir."

"Good, I'll keep my deniability, then. Thank you, Bishou. And thank you for the boost our scholarship fund just got."

What a day, Bishou thought, as she stepped outside. The sun was setting. The atmosphere of the place was different—Friday night on campus. People, mainly couples, were walking around. She could hear subdued, relaxed laughter somewhere in the darkness. But it was not dark enough to disguise the man in the cream-colored suit who waited there.

"What are you doing here?" Bishou asked Louis, walking up to him and looking up into his face.

"You are not in trouble?" Louis asked. "I wanted to make sure you were all right."

"I'm all right."

"Madame Norton said you were at the president's office."

"You've been over to my rooms? You're supposed to be resting."

"Well, I know the way there, now." Even in this dim light, she could see his smile. "We are going on another autobus trip tomorrow. Will you go with us?"

"Sorry, no, I can't. I've got tutoring sessions and a Saturday afternoon class."

"Ah, I am sorry. Then I suppose there is nothing for me to do but return to my hotel room, and sleep. *Si fatigué.*" So tedious.

"No," Bishou said impulsively. "There's a movie playing at the auditorium." She named a James Bond film, *On Her Majesty's Secret Service*, that was making its rounds of the college entertainment centers. "Do you want to go?"

"I would like that," he replied.

They walked across campus to the auditorium. The line had already started to move inside. Bishou reached in her purse for her money.

Louis grabbed her hand, and pushed the purse shut. "What are you doing? *Non.*"

"I invited you," she objected.

"No woman pays my ticket," he replied testily, reaching in his own pocket.

"*D'accord, d'accord,*" she soothed.

They got popcorn, found seats, and got comfortable. "I wish I'd had time to put on slacks," Bishou grumbled, hitching her feet against the empty seat ahead of her.

"You look very nice," Louis reassured her.

They watched previews of forthcoming movies, and then the feature started. Bishou would never have told him she had seen it before—but that was all right, there was plenty she didn't remember. And his reactions were amusing. He jumped when the main character jumped, watched everything carefully, and munched popcorn happily.

They stood outside the auditorium after the movie. "I liked that," he said. "I have always liked action cinema. I am surprised that you do, though. I thought that was a man's weakness. Perhaps it's all those brothers."

"Perhaps so," Bishou agreed with a smile.

"The cinema does not interest you the way it interests me," Louis said. "I suppose I am just a more active nature. I wonder if that is true of most men, that they find joy in these little things?" He tucked her hand around his crooked elbow as they walked. He was comfortable and relaxed in a way he had not been before.

"Maybe you just needed a break from tobacco," Bishou suggested.

"*Oui*. I suppose that is true. Too much of anything is not good for a man. It was good not to think of anything except how the hero was going to catch the villain. And he was a funny hero, not a tragic one. French heroes all seem to die at the end, except a few who merely go to prison." Louis placed his hand over hers, on his elbow. "Your grip changed when I said that. Did you believe I meant myself?"

"No—not really."

"Yes, you did. I did not mean that. I only meant the cinema. What one finds in the prison—that is much different."

"Where were you?" It was tough to grip his elbow and ask that question.

"I almost don't remember. Belleville, after La Santé. The crowding wasn't as bad—and I was not as numb anymore."

"Numb?"

"*Oui. Shoqué*," he affirmed. "It probably—what word?—cushioned me through the worst parts of the experience. And—men are always sympathetic to a man whose downfall was a woman. To be faithful, that means a great deal."

"I wasn't asking about your personal life, Louis, truly I wasn't," Bishou protested.

"No," he said quietly, "I know you were not. I don't know why I wanted to tell you. Except—you said, 'She's beautiful, Louis.' You did not say, 'So that is the evil woman who ruined you, Louis Dessant.' "

"And you are still faithful to her."

"She was my wife," he said simply.

They walked slowly along the darkened paths, in sync, arm in arm. At last, they reached a terrace. Bishou pulled him over to the stone railing, and pointed toward a metal sculpture on the side of a building. The sculpture was lit by spotlights.

"Watch the sculpture," she told him.

"*Hein*? Watch it?"

"Just watch it."

Louis watched, uncomprehendingly, for many long minutes. Then he asked in a puzzled voice, "But it is not the same as when I started watching it—is it?" She heard the boyish laughter again. "It has a motor in it, doesn't it?"

"Yes, it does."

"How pointless! How many people would notice that?"

"They would have to take the time," Bishou replied. "They would need to care enough to look. It is art, beautiful and unexpected. Maybe pointless, too, but I'm not so sure."

"A point one does not understand, or perhaps just not yet."

"You caught my meaning exactly. I find there are many such things in the world. I can't give advice on them. I don't know why they happen, either. But I can like them, and find comfort in them, and befriend them, and maybe some day I will know."

Louis leaned his elbows against the wide stone railing. Then he reached out and clasped her hand. "You will make a good teacher."

"I hope so," Bishou replied seriously.

"And you are strong, *mon amie*."

"I'm not that strong. But if there is only one road to take, well then, I can take that road."

"*Bien dit.* I understand. But sometimes one road is all that is left after making stupid decisions throughout one's life, *hein*?" He stroked her hand. She could feel the roughness of his skin.

"Are you thinking of yourself?" she asked him.

"A little, I admit."

"I wouldn't presume to give you advice, Louis. I really don't know. The only man who gives me advice—at least decent advice, that I might accept—is my brother."

"And yet he allows you to walk on alone."

"If I'm not strong enough, I had better learn. He knows that as well as I do. He's been a Marine in Southeast Asia. All I'm doing is university. It pales by comparison."

"And you are left alone, to make your way in the world."

"*Oui, c'est vrai.*"

"I hope you are not hurt," he said.

"I hope so, too," Bishou replied.

Louis smiled, straightened, and tucked her hand around his elbow, just another man taking his lady home from the movies. They strolled across campus, back toward the graduate apartments.

Walking past a classroom building reminded Bishou of something. "You told Dr. Roth you had met him before, in a lecture hall. When was that?"

"Tuesday morning. Your class."

"You were in the back of my classroom?"

"*Oui.* I wanted to see if you really were a teacher."

"Well! There are no flies on you, Mr. Dessant."

"I did not know enough about universities to know if there were really such people as female college professors," Louis said, "but that showed me, yes."

He had been very matter-of-fact about his interpreter's credentials, she reflected. Now she knew why. He did not take it on faith. For some reason, that made her feel better. She patted his hand. They walked on.

Then Louis broke the silence to say, "Both you and your brother love your useless parents, who make your lives burdens. Why?"

"Why do you love Carola?" she asked.

He did not reply, but acted like that was the answer he expected.

A few yards from the front door of the graduate apartments, he stopped. Louis looked as awkward as she felt. He took her hands in his.

"It has been a long time since I was on . . . a date." It took him a long moment to find the right words. "Thank you for suggesting it. It was . . . nice. If we were not in the middle of a university quad, with students running around us, I might at least kiss your hands."

Bishou chuckled. "I know. And we still have a week of friendship, before we head for opposite sides of the globe. You to run your business, me to look for work. In the meantime, I suppose, we just act like normal people."

This time, Louis chuckled, too. "I suppose. All right. My bus trip tomorrow, then Sunday is free. You might see me then. I do not know." He released her hands. "Goodnight, Bishou."

Louis turned and walked into the darkness. Bishou took a deep breath, and went into the graduate apartment building.

Chapter 9

Saturday absorbed Bishou in work. There were tutoring sessions, student reports to catch up on, and a couple of status reports from teachers who'd given her advisees failing grades. She had back-to-back appointments, with only time out at lunch for a quick sandwich and soda.

At six that evening she dragged herself back to the graduate apartments. Marie Norton was at her door, bottle-feeding the baby.

"Well," Marie greeted her with a grin, "is the weekend starting yet?"

"Three tutoring sessions, three advisee sessions, and two failing-grades." Bishou nodded. "A drink for me and bedtime."

With a jerk of her head, Marie invited Bishou inside. "C'mon in and have the drink with me. Joe's at a night court session, and I haven't seen a grownup in a day."

Bishou really didn't feel like it, but she sympathized. "Deal." She carried her stuff inside Marie's apartment and dropped it on the nearest chair. After a satisfactory burp from the baby, Marie set him down in his crib. Then Bishou and Marie went to the kitchen, poured themselves glasses of wine, and sat at the kitchen table.

"I keep telling myself, just another year," Marie sighed, "but sometimes it's hard."

"I know. Me too."

"People like Louis make it harder, don't they?" Marie flashed her a quick glance.

Bishou sighed, put her elbows on the table wearily, and ran her hands through her hair. "Now, don't you start, too."

"I'm not. I won't. And I admire your iron will, having some myself," Marie said wryly. "But he does, doesn't he?"

Bishou sipped the wine. "Dr. Roth already told me to watch it. He called Louis 'sex in a white package.'"

Marie laughed. "Roth caught that, did he?"

"Mmm-hmm. And the other tobacco people have been trying to fix us up since they got here."

"So forgive me for asking—why isn't it happening?"

Bishou took a deep breath. "I keep reminding them I'm on a job here, and I have to stay professional. They're finally getting used to the fact that Louis Dessant is still carrying the torch for his late wife—which isn't exactly the whole truth, but it's all they need to know."

Quietly, Marie asked, "Am I telling you something you already know if I tell you he has a criminal record?"

Her husband was a lawyer. Joe had looked him up.

Bishou met her gaze. "Yes. Homicide, fugitive from justice, arrested, convicted and found guilty, sentence commuted to seven years at hard labor, released on parole. Now his friends and business have taken him back in, and they're all pretending it never happened. He's trying his best to measure up."

"My God, you don't just erase ten years," said Marie.

"Well, I know that, and you do. I've got a brother who's a Vietnam vet, remember. He's seen people shoot themselves rather than deal with things, just like Louis watched Carola put a gun to her head and pull the trigger." She saw Marie wince. "At least prison wasn't a bad experience for him. He was already so traumatized, he hardly remembers it. Coming back to La Réunion is letting him go through the motions of living a normal life again."

It was Marie's turn to take a deep breath. "Okay, Joe wanted me to ask. I'll tell him I asked."

"I'd appreciate it if you'd both keep this confidential. Short as the conference is, he's still my advisee."

"Of course. But wow."

Bishou smiled. "That's what I thought the first time I saw him. Wow."

"What a hell of a situation you're in, Bishou."

"I'm getting used to it."

***

The next morning was Sunday and Bishou made her way to the chapel. She wasn't religious, but she had promised Bat she would go to church. As she walked across campus, she spotted a man in a dark jacket and grey trousers, walking slowly. Even from the back, she recognized that stance, that hair. Light suit for business, dark suit for Church, she thought. Quickly she walked up beside him and took his elbow. Louis Dessant glanced at her in surprise. Then he tucked her hand around his elbow, and they merged with other nicely dressed attendees of this nondenominational chapel. They found their way to a pew, still without speaking.

Louis knelt on the tiny stool before him, crossed himself, and prayed. Bishou knelt, mainly to be company. She thought about many things, about Bat and his buddies especially. When Louis sat again, she sat beside him. They stood, knelt, sat with the rest of the congregation, and listened to a sermon about peace on college campuses as well as in Viet Nam. Outside the chapel, after the service, Louis observed, "Not many people for a large campus."

"Attendance is optional."

"Why are you here?"

"I promised my brother I would pray for his lost comrades on Sundays."

"A good promise." Louis nodded. He offered his elbow again, and she took it. His rough hand stroked hers. "*Maintenant. Petit dejeuner.*"

"I haven't had breakfast yet, either," Bishou admitted.

"*Bon.* Back to my hotel, then, to their Sunday brunch. Can you bear us all on a weekend, when you thought you would get away from it all?"

"I spent all day yesterday with academic crises. Tobacco people would be a pleasant change."

They talked about his bus tour and her counseling sessions as they walked slowly to the edge of the campus and out a campus gate. Louis asked Bishou, "What do you do with the ones who won't listen?"

"I let them know I understand that they won't, and they must accept the consequences. For most of them, it's their first time away from home, and they're waiting for someone to say, *non, non, cherie*, you must not do that, come back inside. Here, it's not going to happen. They do mess up their lives, and come to me begging for help when it's too late—when their grades are sunk, or they have a child on the way."

"A child. I never thought about that."

"I can't help them. I can give them the address for Planned Parenthood, or counselors, or the suicide hotline—but I can't fake their grades, I can't adopt their babies, I can't explain things to their parents."

"But you can tell them what you see, and warn them. Not that they will listen."

"Not that they will. But a few recognize my warning signs and scramble back onto the path. Those are the ones I'll risk things for, the prodigal sons. Also, the goodie-two-shoes who never leave the path and never seem to be appreciated. I give them a few extra pettings, too."

Louis chuckled. "What would you have told me, if I were truly your advisee?"

"Not a fair question. I can only judge on what I see now."

"What do you see?" He really meant it.

Bishou looked into his eyes. "A man with the respect of his peers, and there must be reason for that. A man with faithful friends, and there must be reason for that, too."

Louis smiled at her, but was not embarrassed. Yes, he'd worked hard to regain the respect and trust he had lost. He just wondered if it showed.

They reached the hotel. Louis escorted her into the lobby, to the brunch buffet. They joined the rest of the tobacco men and helped themselves to a heaping breakfast full of wonderful tastes and smells.

"So were you two off churchin'?" Gray Jackson asked.

"Not together," Bishou replied. "I saw Mr. Dessant along the way."

"Are you a good Catholic?" Sukey asked Louis.

"*Non.* I have fallen from grace. But I go through the motions, nonetheless."

"What do you mean, fallen from grace?" Sukey wanted to know.

Bishou saw how uncomfortable Louis became, and understood. "He means he's broken a commandment or two."

"About half of them," Louis admitted. "I am no longer welcome in a Catholic church."

Vig snorted. "'Bout time you became a Baptist, then. There's nothing wrong with you, Louis."

Bishou kept her nose in her coffee cup. Louis glanced at her, drank his coffee, and kept his silence.

Chapter 10

The week passed rapidly. Monday and Tuesday were full of lectures, tobacco business, and tobacco genetics. They met for lunch. Bishou still taught her Tuesday morning classes, amid tutoring and counseling, and kept a very full schedule.

When they met Wednesday morning, Louis told her, "This is the last day, you know."

She felt a sinking feeling. "I know. I'm sorry. I will miss you."

"And I you, *mon amie*."

There was no denying that last afternoon full of seminars was hard. Everyone felt the end of the conference was near. It seemed like they had always been there, listening to lectures, arguing at lunchtime, and gathering for dinner.

On Thursday morning, Bishou went to the hotel to see off those who were headed for the airport. Louis slid his suitcase into the cargo hold of the bus and turned to her.

"When you have your doctorate, come for the vacation to La Réunion."

"I will be looking for a job after I get my degree in August," she demurred. "I won't be able to afford to travel."

Louis smiled down at her. "Perhaps there will be a tobacco subsidy."

Bishou almost laughed, and admitted, "I know you paid for my work, but still—I wish I could afford to give you your money back."

Louis looked surprised. "Why?"

"Because this was fun, and you are a friend. I didn't feel like an employee."

"You weren't. You let me tell silly stories about Carola and me."

He had, indeed, told her about Carola wanting him to buy a fire-red car, an incident involving taking off her sweater in a public place (braless, yet), about her love of crème de menthe, and other silly little married things that were natural for a widower to mention, but would no doubt have caused Etien to clamp down on him firmly. Louis had been himself, the bereaved husband trying to recover from his loss.

"You made me feel like she was a friend I hadn't yet met," Bishou said. "I rather liked those stories."

Surprised, he smiled again, and clasped her hand in both of his. "Thank you for making me feel . . . normal. Ordinary. Regular."

"You are normal, Louis Dessant, and regular," she answered. "I'm not so sure about ordinary, though."

He squeezed her hand, released it, and climbed onto the bus. The engine started, and she watched it trundle away, out of sight.

"Well," said Gray Jackson's voice, right behind her, "that's that."

She turned and nodded. "That's that. You've run a very successful conference here, Gray." Bishou did not struggle when he put his arm around her shoulder, but slipped an arm around his waist so they could walk back together to the campus. She sensed that it would be easier to work with him than against him. "Why aren't you on the bus?"

"Vig and Sukey live near me. They're giving me a ride home. We've got an extra day."

They walked comfortably together, keeping in step. Gray squeezed her shoulders, to bring her close enough for him to kiss her ear. Then he murmured, "Want to make the most of it?"

"What do you mean?"

"I mean I've got a hotel room here, baby, and everyone else is gone for the day."

"Whoops. That was what I thought you meant, Gray. I'm going to say no even though that is the best offer I've heard in months, and I'm not made of stone, so don't keep asking."

Gray kissed her ear again. "I'll keep asking 'til you say yes, honey. If you can come across for the poor little rich boy, you can come across for me."

This time, Bishou did laugh. "I'm not that kind of girl, Gray, sorry. And what I do is not your business."

"Oh, yeah? What if there's a baby coming, and he's vanished into France? You'd need a man, wouldn't you?"

"If there was a baby coming, I would have a right to be surprised. Because there's only one way for that to happen, and it hasn't happened yet."

"Shee-it," he muttered, in her ear. "You still a good girl?"

"Very good." Another thought struck her. "Goodness. You're jealous. You're jealous, Gray Jackson. You're jealous of Louis Dessant."

"Well, why shouldn't I be?" He sounded indignant. "Waltzes in here with his angel-white suit and hurt-puppy eyes, and does the poor little rich boy thing. And every woman in the state willing to undress for him, goddamn it, while he ignores them and plays the martyr."

Bishou almost argued back in Louis's defense, and caught herself. Why should she tell Gray things Louis himself had not divulged? And why should she be so moody and defensive? Because Gray was right, it was the "poor little rich boy thing" that had caught her attention. As Bat would say, she was acting female. She needed to look at Louis Dessant in a cold light and from a distance— preferably from the other side of her completed dissertation.

Bishou Howard laughed. Her dark cloud dissipated. She stopped walking and turned to Gray. He looked surprised as she placed her hands on either side of his face, and told him, "Gray, I do not want to play around in your hotel room right now. But I would like to buy you a drink. You don't know what it's done for me, to have a handsome fox like you being jealous of yet another sexy male. I will be riding high on that compliment for the next week."

He raised an eyebrow. Then he smiled with good grace. His ego had been salved, too. "As long as you mean the 'handsome fox' part, baby, I'm yours."

"And I mean it. Come on. To the bar, that is."

***

Bishou had let her dissertation slide while the World Tobacco Conference monopolized her life. Now she buckled down to it. She spent early mornings and late nights gathering the materials she needed and compiling her work. Dr. Roth spoke hopefully of a June panel date.

"Do it," she said. "Let's finish this up."

"All right." Sitting once again in Bishou's comfortable easy chair, Roth made a few notes. "What are you going to do after this?"

"For the fall semester? Probably go back to New England, take care of the family, and wait for the word from you. If I have to respond or resubmit, I want to be immediately available."

"Mmm." He nodded. "Going to look for work?"

"Can't, 'til I've got that PhD in hand," Bishou replied reasonably, "unless I want to deal them off the arm in the Exeter Diner."

Roth chuckled. "You can always go into fundraising, according to President Lanthier."

Bishou smiled to herself. "That was a fluke, but yes, I suppose I could do it if I had to."

"Brr. Fundraising gives me shivers, just thinking about it. Okay. I'll get moving on the final rush here, and see what I can dig up for a panel." He rose. "I admit I was a little scared about Louis Dessant. I thought he might drag you from the straight and narrow."

"Not realizing that the event organizer, Gray Jackson, was trying to drag me from the straight and narrow because he was so jealous of Louis Dessant. Thanks, Dr. Roth."

Roth reddened, but he also grinned. "I never spotted that, but it made sense when you told me. Would've been more interesting if he had wanted more than just a drink. I suspect Security would be picking up the pieces and wondering how a man got attacked by a Marine in the middle of campus."

"Gray told me to keep his number in my little black book so I could come cry on his shoulder when Louis Dessant turned me down," Bishou grinned. "I heard Sukey say one day that he's got a woman in every port, and two in some of them. I don't think Gray Jackson is going to suffer long."

Roth eyed her. "I'll bet your number is going to stay in his little black book for a long time, Bishou. You're a bit of a prize, you know. Enough that he didn't want the other guy to get you."

Bishou felt her cheeks burn. "Don't you start, too."

"No more than anyone else," Dr. Roth replied. "I know it's not proper these days to say that a woman thinks like a man, but you do, and maybe that's what saves you. You can't believe they're serious about you." He shook his head. "And yet you dive into all these French works and write commentaries on passion."

"As I said before—writing it, not living it."

"You'll live it, too. You're in the world, Bishou, sometimes too much in it, but in it nonetheless. Yes, you're an academic. And a good one, thank God. But you also see a side of human nature most academics don't experience. You'll be dealing with that dichotomy all your life, I suspect."

"I suspect you're right," Bishou agreed.

Chapter 11

She smiled at the letter with the French stamp, marked ILE DE LA RÉUNION.

Ma chère Mlle. Howard,

Louis has had a good laugh at me, for not realizing you were a woman when I wrote you. My deepest apologies for referring to you as Monsieur Howard. Neither the tone of your letter nor your handwriting gave you away when you contacted me.

Louis speaks well of you. He says that the assistance of someone who was equally comfortable speaking English or French was invaluable to him. He told me the story of the bet, where you explained scientific concepts to a room full of disinterested tobacco growers. It is one of the few times in years that I truly have seen him laugh. You must have amused him greatly!

He also came back with new ideas. Of course, as I told you, I am a cowardly conservative. But he wants to plant some cotton, and experiment with filtered cigarettes, so why not try it? We will see.

Louis is rested and relaxed, more than I hoped for. This American visit did him great good, even if he did have a small nerve-storm in the middle of it. He seems to have recovered from it quite well. I suspect we have you to thank for this.

I know that you are halfway around the world, but it would be a pleasure to meet you someday, and you are always welcome in our home. La Réunion is a beautiful island, you know—a nice place for a vacation.

Regards from both myself and Denise,
Etien Campard

***

Bishou regarded herself in the mirror. White blouse, dark skirt, sensible high heels, and stockings—the female academic outfit the world over. She locked her door as she left, and went downstairs.

"Luck," said Marie Norton, who stood at the door of her apartment as if she had been waiting for her.

"Thanks," Bishou replied.

Bishou walked across campus to a classroom building. Dr. Roth waited outside.

"Are you nervous?" they asked each other at the same moment.

"Jerry Paisley's was yesterday, and Damon King's tomorrow," Roth said, not for the first time, "and there are also sciences panels occurring right now. So we are not alone in our discomfort."

They stood in a corridor until the clock registered 9:00 A.M. exactly. Then, Dr. Roth went inside. A few moments later, he reappeared and motioned Bishou in.

Six men sat at a conference table. Roth took his seat to make it seven. Then the grilling began.

Bishou had already decided not to be upset about obscure questions or star attitudes, both known problems with such panels. She answered questions about her work with a thorough knowledge of it. When a panelist went off on a tangent, she asked for a further explanation, often disclosing a pet peeve that had nothing to do with her dissertation. She never pointed these out; other panelists caught it and moved on. After all, they were busy; there were two of these inquisitions per day, if they were examining literature degree candidates, the most plentiful field.

"God Almighty!" Bishou exclaimed, as she exited with Roth. "We were in there three hours!" Her clothes were soaked with sweat and she felt as if she had spent time playing basketball with her brothers.

"Off you go." Roth patted her shoulder. "I'm taking them to lunch. We'll do a post-mortem some other day. Go home and eat and drink again."

"Right," Bishou said. "See you later."

Back at her rooms, she left the door open and stretched out on the couch. The last summer session had ended; the campus was dead. No one was going to be in this building but her, Marie, and the graduate survivors.

Marie appeared at the door. "Are you still alive?"

"Can't tell yet. I'll let you know after another drink."

Marie sat in Dr. Roth's favorite easy chair. "You won't know the results for another month, will you?"

"No, I won't. Marie, I've been thinking. I'm going to pack up as much of my stuff as I can, sell the crap, buy a used car, and head for home. If I need to come back for responsion, I'll beg a room off you or stay at a hotel. But I can't sit around here for another month during the dead semester, waiting for maybe."

"Sure, makes sense to me. I'll put you up if you have to sleep on the rug—but you won't. I'll bet you don't have a responsion, either, if President Lanthier has anything to say about it. The tobacco people are still sending him donations."

Bishou chuckled. "A good night's sleep. Then I'll deal with this in the morning."

"Goodnight." Marie pulled the door shut.

Bishou closed her eyes and thought of Louis Dessant lying on this couch. That was her only association with this tired piece of furniture. The next grad student could have it, and gladly. The papers, the books—those could go in storage somewhere in New England. Not all the books, even; just the good ones. And her clippings, including the *Gazette* article that had caused so much trouble. Those were keepers.

Bishou closed her eyes, and drifted off to a peaceful sleep—still dressed in her school clothes.

Chapter 12

Bishou knelt on the garden soil and carefully troweled a trench, pulling out some tiny weeds along the way. The day was sunny and bright. She could feel the heat on her bare shoulders. Firmly she planted a tiny onion every three or four inches, and covered it again. There had been a frost in May this year, late even for New England. But now, in June, it was finally safe enough to set out the flats of onions.

Hands rested on her shoulders—oily hands, above the line of the tube top she wore.

"You'll burn if I don't rub this in," said her brother, suiting action to words.

Bat looked like Bishou in the face, enough for them to be dubbed "the twins," and they had the same general body type. But his arms, bare below the T-shirt sleeves, displayed bulging muscles. His dark hair, now grown out, was a scissors cut.

"Thanks. Just because I've been in Virginia doesn't mean I'm used to the sun."

Bat nodded. "Just the heat." He recapped his bottle of suntan lotion. "Feels like you've lost some muscle tone."

"I did. I've been a desk jockey for over a year."

"Put on a little weight, too? Your chest looks bigger."

"If it is, you shouldn't be looking anyway."

He nodded again, unperturbed. "C'mon, I've got beer."

She rose and dusted off the knees of her pants. "Best words I've heard all day."

Bat and Bishou went back into the little house, into the kitchen. He took two bottles of beer from the fridge, opened them, and motioned toward the screened-in porch. Maman sat out there, in her wheelchair, staring out through the screen. Brother and sister kissed her and took seats at the other end of the porch.

Bat propped his legs up on another chair and observed, "Still waiting."

"Not worried." Bishou sipped the good, cold beer. "I did a good presentation. If they didn't like it, that's their pigeon. I can do it again, if I have to."

Bat, still unperturbed, nodded and took a drink from his bottle. Maman, however, wheeled over to scold her daughter.

"You speak as though this weren't the most critical period of your life, Bishou!"

"It isn't, Maman." She smiled into her mother's eyes. "At least, that is what I am telling myself, until the letter comes in the mail. Then, we'll see."

Maman leaned forward, placed her hands on either side of her daughter's head, and kissed her forehead. Then she wheeled back to her previous place at the other end of the porch to stare out at the woods and grasses.

Bat shook his head, ever so slightly. The way the children had discussed everything for years. Wasn't critical. Didn't matter. Not the end of the world, no matter what the parents thought. She nodded, just as slightly.

Bat murmured, "What about Louis?"

She murmured back, "Well, what about him?"

"What you said in your letter."

"One hurdle at a time." She took a sip of the ice-cold beer.

"Gonna look him up?" Bat cocked his head at her.

She frowned, exhaled, did not reply.

"Yeah," said Bat. "You're gone on him."

"Labor intensive."

"And this isn't?"

"And unfair to you. You matter, Brother."

They leaned forward, slapped palms, sat back.

"Don't blow it for my sake," said Bat.

She shook her head. "We had a deal."

"I know. Deals can change." Bat shook a cigarette out of a pack and lit it.

Bishou watched him carefully. "You have a setback?" She watched his eyes as he looked up from his cigarette, and realized for the first time that something was wrong.

"Yes."

"Wanna go for a walk?"

"Can't talk about it yet," he said.

"Good God, Bat." Bishou stared at her brother—the big, muscled, hard-headed Sergeant Major—as if she were seeing him for the first time. He was hurting inside. She stood. "We'll go for a walk anyway."

"I'm not talking."

"Then we'll walk along and say nothing," Bishou said firmly.

Slowly, he stood. His expression never changed, but his body language said he didn't want to do this. They carried their beers with them, told Maman they were going for a walk, and opened the screen door.

They walked along the edge of the backyard, then out of sight through the trees beyond. They headed toward the road, which was quiet on a weekday. They crossed the road, climbed over some guardrails, and went down to a creek bed. The creek was nearly dried up this time of year; there was plenty of space to walk along beside it. They walked upstream for a while, still without speaking.

A bird burst suddenly from a bush, chirping madly. Bat jumped, alert, and watched it flee. *His old reflexes are still there*, she thought. It could have been a sniper.

"I think that's a friendly bird," Bishou said, and Bat grinned.

"Depends on what it drops on us."

She grinned back. "I suppose so."

Bishou did not press him to talk. He would, with time. They moved on.

Much farther upstream he finally sat on a boulder to finish his beer. She sat nearby and did the same.

"So what about this Louis?" Bat asked. "Was he hot?"

She would have told anyone else to mind his own business. "Yeah. Sex in a white package, they called him. The only one who wasn't aware of it was him."

"How come white?"

"Tropical business suit."

"Oh, yeah." Bat tipped up his beer to finish it. "Nice boy?"

"Absolutely."

"Hot for you?"

"No. But some of the other guys were jealous as hell of him anyway, and tried to cut in."

Bat grinned. "Any trouble?"

"Nothing I couldn't handle, thank God." This time, Bat laughed. It occurred to her that she hadn't seen him really laugh lately, and thought: *Neither did Louis.* "Bat, who died?"

The laugh vanished. "Oh, goddamn it."

"No, you didn't give it away. I made an educated guess."

"A chopper pilot."

"Friend?"

He nodded. "Amy MacStay."

"*AMY MacStay?*"

Bat brought his knee up, bunched his fist hard, and placed his mouth against it. *He's trying not to cry,* she realized.

"Oh, goddamn it." Bishou hitched herself up off her rock and put her arms around her brother. She felt him shake, trying to hold in the pain. "No, that's what sisters are for. Let it out."

Bat started to sob, small sobs, still under control. But his face showed agony; eyes clenched tight shut, tears nonetheless. She held him and stroked him.

"That's the problem with you macho men. You don't have practice dealing with meltdowns, especially your own," Bishou murmured.

He sobbed, "Her hitch was almost over."

She understood. They'd been talking marriage. "You always said it's the last three months that get you."

"Yeah. Yeah. And I've held my breath every goddamned mail delivery, worse than you with EVU. Fear that the letter would be there—from her sister, somebody. And it came."

"Any chance she's a POW or something?"

He shook his head. "They got the body. I went to the funeral. Maine." He pulled a filthy handkerchief from his pocket, wiped his eyes, blew his nose, and recovered himself. "Maybe that's why I don't like to see you waiting and waiting, Bishou. Finding excuses for not taking the leap. Saying, just a little longer. It might not be there."

"Louis Dessant jumped in, and look where it got him."

"There's a middle road. You know it. But what I meant . . ." Bat stopped, wiped his eyes, blew his nose again, and began to sound more like himself. "What I meant was, that was my plan, Bishou, marry Amy, move back here near the family, maybe even start a family of my own. And that plan's gone." He snapped his fingers. "You want to run away for a while, you want to travel, I'll cover you. Because I'm sure as hell not going to be doing anything else."

She hugged him closer. "You sound so bitter."

"Why the fuck shouldn't I be? You know and I know it'll change with time. We've both been through this crap before." Bat put his arms around her. "You're a woman, and, Little Sister, you are hot. I may be your brother, but that doesn't mean I have to be stupid about things like that. You want that man, get him. You want that job, get it. Do it."

She pressed his head against her chest. "I want that sheepskin first. Then we'll see what happens. We're just going to mark time for a little while, okay, Brother?"

She felt him nod. "Sounds fair. Family time, what we can get."

"Absolutely. Then I've got to check my finances, too."

"Sell the car."

"I will. But I only have a little cash reserved. I've got to check my assets."

"Got a job as a manager for New England Transit. I'm fixed. I can lend you some."

"Good. I might need it. Don't know what I'm going to do yet, but I'll do something, I promise."

***

A few days later the telephone rang. Bat answered it. "Howard residence." He listened, and then said, "Yeah, Bat, Jean-Baptiste, that's me." A smile started to appear on his lips. Then he said, "Yes, *sir*," and pressed the phone receiver against his shoulder. In his best Sergeant Major's voice, he boomed, "Dr. Roth on the phone wants to speak to Dr. Howard! Front and center, *Doctor!*"

Bishou took the phone receiver from him as her two younger brothers galloped down the stairs. Her father appeared from a corner, looking delighted. Maman wheeled herself in from the porch, looking happy.

"Dr. Roth? Is that you?"

Roth was laughing. "I told the Sergeant Major to make it loud and clear. You'll get your letter in a few days, but I thought I would phone. Will you be able to make it back here the first Saturday in August, for the Conferral of Advanced Degrees?"

"You bet I can," Bishou replied. "I've got to dig up a gown, don't I?"

"I've got it here," Dr. Roth replied. "Your doctoral gown has already been paid for—by a tobacco subsidy."

"Oh, I will be damned," said Bishou. "Not Gray Jackson."

"No, Louis Dessant."

"Louis Dessant?"

"He left the money with President Lanthier before he went back to Réunion Island. The president delegated that little chore of purchasing it to me. Of course, I had no problem, because I knew where I got mine. Come and look us up when you get here. We've got your costume."

"Are you serious?"

"Just come. Third-ever woman doctorate, the place is alight. Expect to be the highlight of the season, Bishou."

"You and me both, Dr. Roth. I'll be there. See you the day before, probably."

"All right. You know the way. We'll see you then."

She hung up, stunned. Her father hugged her. Her mother bade her bend down for a kiss. Bat wrapped his arms around her and asked, "What was that about a gown?"

"Doctoral gown. Mine's already been paid for," she said slowly.

"By the university?" Bat asked.

"No. By the tobacco people. By . . . Louis Dessant."

"As in Dessant Cigarettes?" her father asked in surprise.

"*Oui*, as in Dessant Cigarettes," Bishou replied slowly.

Smiling down at her in his arms, Bat told her, "You may have to go thank him."

"*Oui*, I think I do," Bishou answered.

Chapter 13

Bishou was wearing her "academic uniform" of white blouse, dark below-the-knee skirt, stockings, and sensible high heels when the ferry *Mauritius Pride* docked at the Port of Saint-Denis. She had been through customs at Orly, and these were overseas French departments, so *"Douanes"* was not an issue. She had never understood how anyone could love the scent of the ocean. To her, it always stunk of diesel fuel and dead fish. Then she smiled and chided herself. *Don't run it down, it's Louis and Etien's island.*

Disembarking was bedlam, as bad as a Greyhound bus station in Washington D.C. It was noisy and bright. Passengers got on and off the ferry, cargo was being loaded and unloaded, and plenty of onlookers of all races and nationalities—Africa, India, China, France—gathered around. *This must be the excitement of the day,* she thought.

It all had a very African tone, which she rather liked. It had been that way in Mauritius, too, although the actual twelve-hour ferry ride had been quite peaceful and mellow. One could get a drink at the bar or play cards and chew the fat in a card room. She thought she had spotted a few constant travelers—men and women who worked the ferries, not as paid employees. She could guess how Carola Alese got her start, and the low railings showed easily how she was able to replace an excited mail-order bride on her way to meet her millionaire. Bishou was careful not to talk with strangers about where she was going, and she stayed away from the railings. It was only good sense.

The sky was a beautiful blue. The sun was warm and bright. *Even if I don't get anything out of this trip but a strengthened friendship and a nice job refusal,* Bishou mused, *I'm glad I did it.*

Bishou had asked around the ferry, and had learned that the most visible hotel from the dock, the Harbor Hotel, ought to be avoided. The purser had given her a card for La Pension

Étoile—Star Hotel—a couple of blocks from the dock, along with road directions to it. Without asking, the purser had also told her the story of Louis Dessant, and the criminal who had ruined him.

"But he has been fortunate," the purser said, "if you can call a man who's done time and rehabilitated himself fortunate. He still has friends, a business, and a place where people think well of him. Ah, well," he added, in typical French fashion, "*toujours l'amour*. I don't think too many men will hold that against him."

"And the women?" she had asked with a smile.

"The women? Mademoiselle Bourjois—the sister of the true bride—rides this route at least twice a year, on the anniversary of her sister Celie's death, to warn other young women of the evils of this place. She is so very Paris, the old, mean Paris. *Vous savez?*"

Bishou nodded; she did know.

"But other women, they take autobus rides near the factory, just on the hope of seeing the poor, desolated man. *Par Dieu m'en faire*—pardon, Mademoiselle!" he said, as she started to laugh at the French obscenity. "I forget, your brother is a soldier, you've probably heard worse."

She thought of Bat now, recommending a backpack over a heavy suitcase, and insisting she get back into shape before this trip. Bishou stumped firmly up the cobbled streets, blessing him for his foresight. In the distance, she saw a blue star on a sign and guessed that was La Pension Étoile ahead.

It was. She stepped inside a cool, white lobby, where two genteel middle-aged ladies stood at the desk, signing in some other new arrivals. She waited until the current (and apparently well-known) customers were taken care of, and then stepped up to the counter.

"*Bonjour*, Mesdames," she said to them in French, passing the card across the counter. "Monsieur Martin of the *Mauritius Pride* recommended you highly."

"Ah, *bonjour*, Mademoiselle?" There was a question in the tone.

Bishou smiled her acknowledgment. "*Oui*, Mademoiselle Howard. I am *étrangère* here, a visitor."

"Ah. Welcome. And what brings you to our lovely island?" asked one lady.

"I wanted to see it, because I have heard so much about it. I am also applying for work, at the university, while I am here."

"Oh, how exciting!" the other lady said. "Are you a secretary?"

"No, a teacher."

"Oh, Mademoiselle. I do not wish to disappoint you—our university is just starting, so I could be mistaken—but all those teachers will be college professors, you know, not schoolteachers."

Bishou gave them her gentlest smile. "Actually, I am a college professor, too. Docteur Bishou Howard, professeur de littérature, Université de Virginia de l'Est, des États-Unis." It was the first time she could remember introducing herself that way, especially in French.

"Oh, goodness!" the ladies exclaimed, or words to that effect. "A woman! And an American! Here!"

"Don't say anything, though. It could be bad luck. You know how job applications are."

They probably didn't, but they nodded sagely. Then it occurred to them they hadn't even filled in a hotel form for her yet, and got to work. She paid for three days, cash.

Their porter, an elderly Creole, insisted on taking the backpack for her. Upstairs, she tipped, half what she would pay in Paris but double the rate here; he smiled broadly and touched his hat. Stowing her backpack in the room's wardrobe, she stopped him to ask a question. French was the school language, so even the oldest Creoles spoke it, although badly. "Where do I go to catch the bus?"

"Don't Mam'selle want nice taxi?"

"No, *mon ami*. Mam'selle wants to see green trees and smiling faces, and go slow."

The smile got broader. "You go down to Missy's bodega, take a left out here and two blocks down. Corner store—you know?"

"*Oui*. I know bodega."

"Bus stop too. Driver be Armand, this time of day, good fellow. Tell him Joseph sent you, give him cigarette maybe."

"Does he like Dessants? That's all I'm carrying."

His smile got even broader. "Everybody like Dessant. This his island."

"That's what I heard," she agreed with a smile. "*Merci*, Joseph."

"You teach a few words American?"

"Thank you, Joseph, you are kind," she said, in English.

"Thank you, Mam'selle, you are kind." He grinned, touched his cap, and left.

Bishou tucked her room key in her pocket and strapped her purse firmly across her shoulder. Then she followed directions to the corner store. A Creole woman worked busily behind the counter.

"Cigarettes?" asked Bishou.

"What brand?" the woman said busily.

"Dessant," Bishou replied, as if that were obvious.

The woman stopped, and grinned at her. "Sorry if I was rude, Mam'selle."

"You weren't. Are you Missy?"

"*Oui*, I am."

"Joseph at Pension Étoile said this was the best store in town."

Missy grinned, showing some missing teeth. "He should. He owes me money." The woman grinned in pleasure as Bishou laughed at the joke. Quickly she took Bishou's bills, and gave her change. "Now, what else can I do for you, Mam'selle?"

"Tell me about the bus. Where it goes, when it comes."

"I've got a schedule here." She slid one across the counter. "You can keep that."

"*Merci*. I just want to ride around and see things. *Je suis étrangère*."

"A good plan, in a new place." Missy nodded. "You come from Mauritius?"

"*Oui.*"

"And before then?" Missy was distracted by the appearance of another customer, then by the beep of the bus. "Autobus, Mam'selle. This is what you want."

"*Merci,*" said Bishou, running outside before Missy could ask any more questions.

Now she saw what Louis meant about Réunion buses. This bus had sort of a roof, but there were seats all around the outside, too, and its top speed was probably ten kilometers per hour, downhill. She followed the lead of the others, paid the driver, and found a seat. She sat inside the bus, near him, though.

"Are you Armand?" she asked.

The driver replied, "Joseph sent you?"

Bishou dumped a few cigarettes into her hand, and passed them to him. He grinned with delight.

"He said, Armand likes those Dessant cigarettes, Mam'selle, so give him some. And he will tell you everything you want to know."

Other passengers around them, mainly Creole but some French, watched and smiled.

The driver grinned again and shifted into gear. The bus was not quite as loud as a lawnmower, but moved at about the same speed. "Where do you want to go, Mam'selle?"

"I just want to see some of the region, and come back to Missy's."

"Just right," said the driver. "That's my route. That makes it a three-hour trip, *d'accord?*"

"*D'accord,*" she nodded. By then, it would be almost nightfall, a good time to get back to the hotel and try to sleep.

Joseph pointed out museums, banks, the retail area, and libraries as they started through town. "And those buildings over there, that's the new Université Française de l'Océan Indien, our own university," he said proudly. "Just started about five years ago."

"I'm going to go there when I get older," said a little Creole boy in the opposite front seat. His mama brushed his hair with one hand.

"I think that is a good plan," Bishou told the little boy. "Then you can learn much, and maybe work in a business like a bank or publishing house."

Her acceptance of the little boy made a difference in the atmosphere around her. This went from a silent bus to a bus full of quiet conversations, as they talked with the strange woman. Mainly, as Joseph pointed out more landmarks, they elaborated on his description, even if it was just to say "I was baptized in that church."

There were no suburbs in Saint-Denis—one moment you were in the city, the next you were riding down one-lane dirt roads, past occasional farms.

Joseph pointed. "That's the Dessant Cigarette factory over there."

"I saw tobacco fields all around us," she commented. "It's big."

"*Oui*. Monsieur Dessant is a rich man."

"But a nice man," another woman interrupted. "So is Monsieur Campard, his partner."

"And they are *réunionnais*," said a man.

"Oho," said Bishou. "That is it, is it not? They are family. Family protect their own."

Everyone within hearing range started to laugh, some almost sheepishly.

"That is how it is," agreed Joseph, laughing too. He pointed down another road. "That is Rue Dessant, where Monsieur Dessant's house is. Far over there—you can barely see it—is the road to Rue Calaincourt, where Monsieur Campard's house is.

The tour buses, they go there. But I stick to the main road. I have to stay on schedule. Else I would show you their beautiful houses."

"That's all right. I have seen other beautiful houses," Bishou said. "I enjoy more seeing people. The best part of my voyage, so far, has been the people I have met."

"Are you a tourist, then, mam'selle?" Joseph asked her.

"*Oui.* Seeing friends, and maybe applying for work while I am here. I am not rich, so I must be very careful with my money."

"And then what?"

"Then whatever job I obtain," she answered.

"Well, good luck," said Joseph. "I hope you'll be commuting on this bus in the afternoon, Mam'selle."

"I hope so, too," she replied.

Chapter 14

Bishou's travel alarm clock chirped her awake. She had been dreaming of the easygoing, almost idyllic ride yesterday, and woke up comfortably in the bright sunlight. Eight o'clock. Time to train her body out of the jet lag—the *décalage*, as Louis had called it. Strange, how peaceful she felt.

Bishou changed out of her pajamas and went to the bathroom at the end of the hall to wash up and brush her teeth. *This pension is so very French*, she thought. In another day, she was going to have to barricade the bathtub and take a soak—she hadn't had a thorough wash since Mauritius. Then she smiled to herself. She was even thinking like Bat. She'd ask them if she could bathe today, while everyone else was out.

When she went downstairs, she heard the two sisters talking before she appeared, and she could smell coffee. The ladies were very excited to see her. "Oh, Mademoiselle, *venez, venez!*" They almost bodily brought her through a doorway behind the hotel desk. To her astonishment, breakfast awaited: Croissants, orange juice, coffee. Amazingly, too, they sat down with her, and plied her with questions about America. Between mouthfuls, Bishou talked about New England, Virginia, her handsome brother Jean-Baptiste, her coed years.

"And you traveled without chaperone?" one asked, staring in surprise.

"Certainly."

"But suppose a man tried to attack you?"

"My brother is a soldier. He insisted I learn to defend myself."

"Oh! Have you ever used the lessons you learned?"

"Well—yes. But most of the time, I talk my way out of trouble."

These middle-aged spinsters giggled like teenagers as they talked with Bishou about wandering all around America. It was a concept they couldn't imagine, anymore than they could imagine a 10,000-kilometer voyage—it could just as well be a science-fiction movie to them. In fact, the cinema was more real—there were three cinema houses in Saint-Denis alone.

The croissants, coffee with lots of cream and sugar, and juice kept coming. Bishou almost had to hide her coffee cup to prevent a "freshening up."

"*Non, non, non*! I will be as fat as a goat if I let you have this cup again, Mademoiselle!" she protested, as they all laughed. "Besides, I have things I want to do today."

"Well, if it is shopping, Docteur," said the other sister, "remember, the shops close from noon to two. And it is almost ten, now."

"*Non, non*. I will tell you later." Bishou rose. "*Au revoir*. And some time, I must repay you for this lovely meal."

Once outside, she walked again to Missy's, greeted her briefly, and took a bus with a different driver, a morning bus. "*Université*," she told him.

He merely nodded, and took her money. She sat on the outside. When the bus slowed down at the *université*, she simply dropped off and walked up to the gates. Bishou stepped through the open gates and found herself in a small quadrangle. Some things were universal. She found the public jobs board, read it, and smiled.

Bishou located the College of Humanities building. Entering, apparently at class-change time, she worked her way through the throngs of students to the office. The secretaries were busy, so she took a seat. She could wait. When the last student was finished at the desks, she approached a secretary. *Talk about universal*, Bishou thought, at the woman's hostile glance up at her, through half-glasses on a chain.

"*Bonjour*, Madame. I wish to speak with Dr. Rubin. Is he available?"

"*Doyen* Rubin," she emphasized the word for dean, "is busy with students. May I help you?"

"Yes, I am looking for work. I sent him a letter."

"Then you should go to University Administration, Mademoiselle. The dean is not in the habit of hiring secretaries," she said with asperity.

"No doubt he is not. But I understand his word is vital in hiring professors of literature," Bishou said calmly. "Would you ask him if he could please make time to meet Dr. Bishou Howard?"

Her jaw dangled. "*Docteur* Howard?"

"*Oui*, Docteur Howard."

"I—he—it may be a few minutes before I can interrupt him, Docteur."

"*D'accord*," said Bishou agreeably. "I'll wait."

She sat down again in a rickety old chair and flipped through a stack of ancient magazines. From the corner of her eye, she saw the consternation of the secretarial pool as they realized the woman waiting in the corner was a professor. Then she heard the rapid clicking of heels as a secretary headed down a corridor. A few minutes later, the heels clicked back again, and returned to Bishou.

"Pardon, Madame—I mean, Docteur," she said. She held a clipboard. "*Le doyen* asked that you fill out these forms, *s'il vous plâit*."

"Surely." Bishou took the board from her and slid a pen out of her purse. The secretary left, almost superstitiously, and retreated to her desk.

One of the forms was a plain old job application, but—she smiled as she looked at some of the others—there were insurance forms, pension forms, and so on, the forms of someone who had already been hired.

The dean had pulled the forms from the file he'd already started on her, and given them to the secretary to pass on. The Journal of Higher Education had been correct when it said this school was new, and the jobs board had said they were desperate for new hires in a few significant areas, including comparative literature. Dr. Rubin already had her résumé. She had sent it with her letter from the States. In compliance with U.S. law, and also with the newest French laws, none of the paperwork had happened to mention that she was a woman. There was probably a lot of retrenching going on in that back office.

Bishou was copying her passport number onto one of the forms when a shadow fell over it. She looked up to see the Frenchest Frenchman she'd ever seen, spectacles and little goatee and all, frowning down at her. "Dr. Howard?"

"*Oui.*" She slipped her passport back in her purse, and stood with the clipboard.

"I am Dr. Rubin."

"It is a pleasure to meet you, Monsieur le Doyen," she said. She put out a hand before he did, and they shook hands.

"Please, come into my office."

He motioned for her to precede him, but she shook her head and motioned to him. After all, he knew the way. And he was the dean. He led the way back to his office, a reasonably sized enclosure with a glass door. He closed the door and slid behind his desk. They sat down simultaneously.

"Well, Docteur," he said. "What brings you to our beautiful island?"

"I just received my doctorate, Monsieur le Doyen, and now I need experience. The climate of Réunion Island is much like Virginia, and you had a job opening in the very area in which I have taught—comparative literature."

"I saw that you spent time studying in Paris." He was re-reading her resume. "But how do you speak French so well?"

"My family is French-Canadian," Bishou replied. "My father is now retired, but he was a professor in Massachusetts." She named the three universities at which Dad had taught. "My mother was a teacher in a college preparatory school." She named the school, which was also well known. "My brothers and I switch easily between the French and English tongues."

They spoke back and forth a while longer. During this time, Bishou "happened to mention" that she taught freshman classes, she taught early hours, she tutored, and she had assisted with fundraising. Dr. Rubin never came out and said it was an all-male, all-French faculty, but she got the gist. He also "happened to mention" that women's salaries weren't as high as men's, and she "happened to mention" that a doctorate was a doctorate. No blood was shed, but the battle lines were drawn.

"Would you be willing to give a presentation some evening?" he asked.

"*Bien sûr,*" she replied. "On what topic? Passion in literature, my dissertation topic? Or do you have a favorite subject of your own?"

He smiled a stiff smile, and gestured away the topic. "Réunion thrives on different passions."

"So I have been told," she said, and did not smile.

He gave her a calculating look. "How long will you be here?"

"I do not know yet. A week, perhaps."

"Where are you staying?"

"La Pension Étoile," she replied.

"Ah, not a private home," he said, a leading question if ever there was one.

"Non, Monsieur le Doyen."

"That is expensive, is it not?"

"*Oui,* it is." She said no more, not wanting to give him an opening to delay his decision until after she would be forced to leave. She knew that academic delay tactic, too.

"I must meet with the college president, and then arrange the presentation," he said. "I will be in touch with you."

"*Merci,* Monsieur le Doyen," Bishou said, understanding that the appointment was over.

She stood as he did. Yes, they did have good timing together—that was a positive sign. She let a smile touch the corner of her mouth, just barely, and thought she saw a twinkle in his eye. It was too early to judge, though.

He walked her to the front office. "Give your paperwork to Mme. Ellis," he said, indicating the secretary who had first greeted her. "She will take care of it." They shook hands, as the secretaries stared at them. "*Au revoir*, Dr. Howard."

"*Au revoir*, Monsieur le Doyen," Bishou replied. Then she turned to the secretary. "Madame, I have not finished this paperwork. Do you mind if I return to the corner, to work on it?"

"Go ahead, Docteur," said Mme. Ellis politely.

Bishou finished the paperwork, and returned to the secretary's desk with the clipboard. She was aware that she would be the most-talked-about event of the secretarial pool for the next three days, at least. "*Voici*, Madame. And thank you for your help."

"*De rien*, Docteur. *Au revoir*."

Back out in the sunlight, Bishou checked her watch. It was half-past eleven, not yet siesta time in Saint-Denis. She walked to the front gate, trying to decide whether to travel farther or return to the pension for a bath and a nap. The bus was waiting there. She made her decision. She would travel farther.

She climbed aboard. "Rue Calaincourt," she told him, as she paid her fare.

The driver merely nodded, and the bus trundled on its way.

At the Rue Calaincourt stop, several passengers disembarked. They headed elsewhere, not up the Rue itself. Bishou walked it alone.

There were two pretty houses along the way, but neither was number 7. A third house on the left—stuccoed, earth-toned, shingle-roofed, clean and neat—struck her as a possibility. She turned up the front path. The windows were open, so surely her footsteps were audible to anyone who might be at home. She smiled at a tiny "7" painted on the exterior, near the front door.

The door opened before she reached it. A bespectacled woman, hardly much older than Bishou, stood there. "Oh, *mes apologies*. I thought the children were early. What may I do for you?"

"Madame Campard?"

"*Oui*," she replied curiously.

"I am called Bishou Howard."

Denise Campard stared. Then she screamed, and threw her arms around Bishou's neck.

Bishou smiled, and returned the hug. "Does this mean you recognize my name?"

"Oh! Oh! Oh! *Recognize* it?" Her cries had brought the Creole housekeeper running. Denise waved her off with one hand. "*Non, non, non,* Josie, it's all right—oh, it's not all right, it's wonderful, Josie, make us some coffee, will you? Recognize the name? Oh, come in, come in! Welcome! You, of all people, in our home!" She grabbed Bishou's hands, and dragged her into the living room. "What are you doing here, Bishou? Have you come to see Louis?"

"*Non*. I haven't seen him yet. I wanted to see you both first—to see how he was, and to see if it was a good idea."

"Good idea?" She sounded incredulous.

"Well, you know, he collapsed at my place."

"You're the only woman he ever mentions, besides his secretary and Carola." To her credit, Denise Campard did not make a face when she said Carola's name. "You'll stay for lunch, won't you? How did you get here? Where are you staying? Oh, you just dropped out of the sky! Louis said he couldn't write you anymore at East Virginia University, and then you left New England, your brother wrote to tell him."

"What else did my brother say?" she asked curiously.

"Just that he didn't know your plans. Louis was disappointed that there was no forwarding address in your brother's note. Oh, to think that you should be here!" She hugged Bishou again. "Oh,

I must tell Etien. No, I won't have to. He'll be home for lunch in a few minutes. He'll bring the boys. You'll have lunch with us, then?"

Bishou was still smiling. "Of course I will. I've wanted to meet all of you for so long."

"*You* wanted to meet *us*? *Mon Dieu!*" Denise exclaimed. "Oh, wait, wait, I hear the car. Oh, *viens, viens.*" She almost dragged Bishou bodily to the entryway.

They heard boys' voices, laughter, and their father's replies. Then the front door opened. A thin, bespectacled businessman in a suit, with a schoolboy on either side, stared in surprise at his wife who rested an arm around another woman.

"*Bonjour,*" said Etien Campard courteously, looking questions at his wife.

"Etien," said Denise, "*voici* Bishou."

Etien Campard dropped his briefcase. Stunned, he stepped forward and hugged her. "Oh, *mon Dieu.* Bishou."

"*Bonjour, mon ami,*" she said in his ear, returning the hug. "I am so glad to meet you at last."

"What are you doing here?"

"Meeting you. Making sure Louis is all right. Traveling before I start working at a full-time job."

He pulled back enough to look at her. "Louis said you received your doctorate."

"Yes, I did."

"And now you are free of your obligations in America?"

"*Oui,* I am."

A smile lit up his face. "I am glad to hear that."

Denise dragged them all to the lunch table. The boys started asking the strange lady questions. They were interested to hear that she had two younger brothers and an older one, in America. Did they have a dog? Had she ever seen an Indian? Did she climb on the Rocky Mountains? Their questions seemed childish—the boys were almost the same ages as her younger brothers. Then she thought, *No, my brothers have aged before their time.*

"So Louis does not know you are here," said Etien.

"Etien! Let's surprise him," said his wife.

"I'm not sure about that," Bishou objected. "I don't want him to faint again."

"That was stress and exhaustion," Denise said. "He's at home now, having lunch. Why don't we invite him to come over?"

"Yes! Let's surprise Oncle Louis!" said Jean-Luc, the elder son.

"I don't know," said Bishou. "Don't you think it will upset him too much?"

"*Non!*" said the younger boy, Pierrot. "Not Oncle Louis. Besides, we'll be here to take care of him."

"Are you going to marry him?" Jean-Luc asked.

The parents looked shocked at such a loaded question, but Bishou understood how young boys' minds worked. "Why, do you think he needs someone to take care of him?"

"*Bien sûr,*" Jean-Luc replied. "He's got Bettina the housekeeper and Madeleine the cook, but they don't keep a really good eye on him."

"He gets sick," Pierrot contributed, "and Papa and Maman worry about him."

"It's difficult, isn't it?" she agreed. "My brothers and I have to worry about our parents the same way. They are very sick. My maman is in a wheelchair."

"Really? A wheelchair?" Pierrot's eyes grew as big as saucers. "Do you push her around?"

"Sometimes. But she knows how to turn the wheels herself, too."

"Wow. Is there snow where you live?"

"Yes, there is. We go hiking and skiing in it."

"Wow," said the boys.

Etien's eyes twinkled as he realized that Bishou understood the children's questions, and was not embarrassed. "Now. What do we do? Do we telephone Oncle Louis?"

"Yes!"

"And what do I say? I am not a good liar."

"Tell him that we have something for him, and it just arrived on the ferry," his wife suggested. "That is close enough to the truth. And we did have him over for a little party, two weeks ago, when he turned thirty-six. Let him think it's a late present."

"He'll look in the window, rather than knock. He always does."

"The boys will hide in the bedroom with Bishou. They can sneak up on him once he sits down at the table."

"We are sure to give it away."

"Well," said Bishou, "if we do, then we can be sure he won't faint, yes?"

Etien grinned. Denise giggled. Etien rose, went to the telephone, and dialed a number.

After a pause, he said, "Bettina, *c'est* Etien Campard. May I speak with Monsieur Dessant, please? *Allo*, Louis? Can you come over? There's something here at the house, just arrived on the ferry, that I want you to see. I may need some help with it. *Non, non*, it's hard to describe. You will see. Come and have coffee with us, too. *Bon*, ten minutes. *Au revoir*." Etien hung up. "Ten minutes."

"I heard," said Bishou.

The boys led her into their parents' darkened bedroom, just off the living room. They all squatted down beside the bed.

"Ssh, ssh!" they whispered, giggling, "or he'll hear us."

The boys gripped her arms tightly when they heard a car arrive, the sound of footsteps, and Louis's voice. Then Bishou heard Etien Campard opening the front door, and Louis stepping inside.

"Well, what is this thing, Etien?" Louis Dessant asked his partner.

"I'll show you in a bit. Come have some coffee." Etien led him to the dining area.

Bishou and the children peeked out the bedroom door to see a man dressed in white, his back to them, seated on a dining room chair.

Louis exchanged greetings with Denise, who poured coffee, made sure he had cream, all the little things one does for a guest.

Bishou whispered to the boys, "You must go out and say hello, and distract him. Make sure he does not look behind him, and I will sneak across."

The boys, grinning, ran out. "*Boujour*, Oncle Louis!"

"*Bonjour, mes enfants!*" he greeted them cheerfully. "What is this surprise, do you know?" He was nonplussed when both boys giggled.

"Jean-Luc, Pierrot, you come and sit down over here, beside me," their mother interposed.

"Oh, Maman, I will stay here—"

"Come," she said firmly, while Etien wiped a grin from his face and sat down beside his partner. Jean-Luc continued standing behind Louis's left shoulder, trying hard not to giggle.

"Jean-Luc, you are up to something," Louis said, suspicious.

Etien poured cream into Louis's coffee and appeared calm—although he couldn't hide the twinkle in his eye. The atmosphere in the room seemed almost electric.

Bishou made an exaggerated business out of sneaking up behind Louis. Denise tried hard not to look, and failed. One boy was giggling, the other was clenching his jaw. Louis could tell that something was happening behind his back. When he started to turn around, Jean-Luc put his hands over Louis's eyes.

"Oh, *non*, Oncle Louis, don't turn your head!"

"You'll spoil the surprise," Etien concurred. Etien's assurance made Louis stop and sigh.

"You monkeys are up to something," he said.

"*Oui*, they are," Etien agreed, "but I think it's a surprise you will like."

"I don't like surprises. At all. Ever," said Louis flatly.

She was close enough, now, to nod to Jean-Luc. He slid his hands away from Louis's eyes, and she slid hers into place.

"All right," said Etien, in that same reasonable voice. "Guess the surprise."

Louis touched the hands over his eyes, felt a woman's fingernails. He felt her left wrist, and the lady's watch she wore. He touched the college ring on her right hand.

"*Une bague*—"He stood up like a shot, and spun around, staring at her. At last, he spoke. "Bishou?"

"*Oui*, Louis."

"Bishou." Louis pushed the chair aside. He reached out and drew her closely. He closed his eyes, and pressed his face into her hair. "Bishou."

She wrapped her arms around his neck. "*Oui.*"

His voice was soft and disbelieving. "How can this be? You are in America. You are half a world away."

"*Non*, I am right here."

"Ah, *non*," he said, pressing his face into her shoulder, "I am hallucinating again."

"*Aussi*," she said. Me, too.

Smiling, Etien asked Louis, "Well. Was it worth the trip over here?"

*****

They sat on the couch while Louis tried to recover himself. When he could form sentences again, he asked, "But why are you here?"

They still held hands. "I came to see how you were doing," she told him.

"But Etien could have told you that," he gently protested.

"Etien only says what he wants me to hear."

"Well, that is true," Louis agreed in amusement, watching the indignant look on Etien's face. "But it is all for the best, you know. That is what he would tell us." An anxious look appeared. "Your degree, it is all right, is it not?"

"Of course it is. Do you want to see it? It's in my luggage in the hotel room."

"Hotel room? Friends on this island, and you stay in a hotel room? Etien?"

Apparently, Etien had the same thought. "Stay here, Bishou."

"*Non*. It wouldn't be right to stay with either of you. The hotel it is."

"If you say so," Louis said grudgingly. "I would not waste my time and energy arguing with you. I know better." He released her hand. "Now, tell me how you came here."

Bishou drank some of Denise's coffee. "Well. After the World Tobacco Conference ended, I finished my dissertation. In June, I defended it against the examining panel, and waited at home with my family to see if I would need to prepare a responsion."

"Responsion?"

"Response to objections to my thesis. But no, it went through without too much difficulty, *grâce à Dieu*. Dr. Roth telephoned even before I got the official letter."

"Congratulations!" Etien said heartily.

Louis still watched her carefully. "But then something happened," he prompted.

She glanced at him, wondering how he could possibly know that.

"Your plan was to seek work in America, and take your brothers off Bat's hands. That did not happen. Why not?"

She sighed and looked for words. "Bat told me he wanted to stay on at home, and told me to travel."

"Told you?"

"*Oui*, told me. Things are not good with Bat," she said in a very restrained voice.

Louis patted her leg, and dropped the subject. "How are you dealing with exhaustion and *décalage*?" he asked, with an impish grin.

"Terribly. I can feel myself falling asleep, even now. And I do so need a bath." Bishou stood. "Let me go back to the hotel and sleep. Perhaps I can see you, tomorrow afternoon?"

Louis also stood. "I will drive you back."

"No, you won't," said Etien, also standing. "If you drive a young lady back to Pension Étoile, Louis, those old birds will gossip for a week."

"And if you do it, they will say Etien Campard has not only a wife, but a mistress," Louis returned. "Stay out of trouble, will you?" There was a little volley of friendly half-insults, but Louis eventually won his point. He escorted Bishou outside, where a neat little Mercedes convertible, top down, waited behind a yellow Panhard. Louis held the door for Bishou to get into the white convertible. *Of course,* thought Bishou, *it would be white.*

They drove as slowly as the autobus, down the narrow dirt path and back to the equally narrow main road. Even the road was green, half-covered with grass.

"I've never ridden in a Mercedes before," said Bishou.

"Really?" He shifted gears and glanced at her in surprise. "Are there not many in New England?"

"*Non.* They're diesel, and don't start well in cold weather."

"Only you, Bishou, would know the man's reason why no one owns the car. A woman would be more likely to say it is not pretty, or it is not very comfortable." Louis glanced at her as she leaned back to look at the trees and the sky. "I am so glad to see you, *mon amie.* I cannot quite persuade myself yet that you are real."

She closed her eyes, letting the sun beat upon her face and the wind blow through her short hair. Birds chirped. A distant animal hooted. "I'm real, Louis."

He kept his eyes on the road. "So I see. I will pick you up tomorrow afternoon, around three. Is that agreeable to you?"

"I will be ready," she promised.

It took about twenty minutes for him to reach the pension. There was not much traffic, but he did not hurry. She was half-asleep when they arrived.

Louis reached out and touched her shoulder. "Ah. Are you asleep?"

"No. But I was drifting off. Thank you for the ride, Louis."

Louis got out and opened the car door for her. She gave him her hands, and he clasped them. He gazed into her eyes.

"It is still a dream," he said. "I will know for certain if I come here tomorrow, and you are not here. And never have been."

Bishou smiled. "I'll be here, Louis."

"Promise me?"

"I promise."

She watched the white car drive off. *He still doesn't believe I'm real*, she mused. *He expects to have the rug yanked out from under him.*

The pension was nearly empty, a good time to take a bath. She bathed and washed her hair. The warm bathwater made her so sleepy that she returned to her room, donned her pajamas, wound her little traveling clock, climbed into bed, and fell asleep.

Chapter 15

The deep horn of the *Mauritius Pride* as it docked told her it was morning even before she opened her eyes. She had slept the day through, and the night. Her little alarm clock said eight o'clock. She got up, found fresh clothes, and made her way to the bathroom at the end of the hall. After that, she went downstairs.

The sisters greeted her. "We tapped on your door last night, and never a sound," said the elder sister, Eliane. "I hope you don't mind—I used my passkey to look in and make sure you were all right."

"I don't mind. Was I snoring?" Bishou asked with a grin.

"Perhaps a little," Eliane admitted.

"You were certainly exhausted," the other sister, Marie, commented. "Come, come, we still have some coffee and croissants."

They led her in behind the counter, back to their own area, and sat her down.

"Now," said Eliane, patting her knee. "Was that Monsieur Dessant who brought you home?"

"*Oui.* He is an old friend."

"He is? Where did you meet him?"

"I was a translator at East Virginia University when he attended the World Tobacco Conference there."

"I thought he spoke English," said Eliane.

"Yes, he does, and very well. But he was not certain his knowledge of English would be enough for an entire conference, so he hired someone through the university to assist him—me."

"Oh, how exciting!" Marie exclaimed. "But, you know, he has a reputation, do you not?"

"Reputation? How so?" Bishou pretended she did not know.

"He did a very foolish thing in his younger days," said Eliane.

Marie pooh-poohed her elder sister. "But it was so romantic, and how was he to know? He arranged for a mail-order bride, and

126

fell in love with her at once when she arrived. She was incredibly beautiful, Mademoiselle. I remember seeing her. And the wedding! The entire island was there, I think."

Eliane took up the tale, frowning. "And she turned out to be a criminal. She and her lover had murdered the real bride. She broke away from her lover, and ensnared Louis Dessant instead. Monsieur was so entranced; he even killed a detective to protect her."

"And they ran away, throughout France," Marie cut in. "They were on the run for at least a year. And when the police finally caught them, she killed herself—right before his eyes—rather than be arrested. She knew how evil she was. But poor Monsieur Dessant, he was taken."

"He paid for their crimes," Eliane said sternly. It was difficult to tell her actual feelings from her expression.

"How did he end up, back here?" Bishou asked, wondering how they would respond.

"This is his island," Marie replied. "He is one of us. We wouldn't let him down."

Those words rang in her ears as she wandered down the streets of Saint-Denis. *He is one of us, we wouldn't let him down.* Not much different from her family, really.

Bishou stopped before a dress shop. Sundresses hung in the window. If she stayed in Saint-Denis much longer, she might have to get one. Her own clothes felt so hot. Another shop window displayed high-heeled shoes. Sexy, feminine, attractive ones, the kind she never wore. Another store was a jewelry shop. Skip that. The next was a bridal boutique. *Skip that, too,* she told herself.

Bishou bought coffee at a little café, and sat at a table on the sidewalk. *Very Parisian,* she thought. When she finished her coffee, she continued on toward the université. As she crossed the street to enter the université gates, a little yellow car cut her off. Startled for a moment, she realized the car was a Panhard. Driving it was Etien Campard.

He was not smiling. "What are you doing here, Bishou?"

She slid in beside him. "Why are you here, Etien?"

He pulled over to the curb, parked, and shut off the engine. "Answer my question, Bishou, please."

She regarded him with surprise. "Etien, why are you upset?"

"I want to know what you are doing in this part of town."

Suddenly, Bishou understood. She was touched.

"Etien." She smiled. "Let me show you. Come, get out of the car." When he hesitated, she repeated, "*Viens.*" Come. In the tense of a friend.

Unwillingly, Etien got out of the car. Even more unwillingly, he took her hand. She clasped it firmly, and drew him across the road. They entered the université gates and she took him to the "Jobs Board," as it was known in America, and showed him the posting.

Etien read the notice, at first uncomprehendingly—an advertisement for a tenure-track professor of comparative literature, and the job's requirements. Then he started to smile with relief. "You qualify."

Bishou nodded. "And I need the practice. I don't have any teaching experience since I received my doctorate, just pre-doctorate experience. I had an interview with the *doyen* yesterday. I was just coming back to remind them. Even though I am a woman, and I shocked them severely. They didn't know I was female until they met me yesterday. Getting the job might be my greatest struggle."

"A college professor?" Etien reread the notice. "It says part-time."

"I know it does. Starting positions often are."

She felt the difference in his grip. "I'm sorry I . . ." Etien stopped, searching for words.

Softly, Bishou said, "It was you who saw warning signs about Carola, wasn't it? And you've never forgiven yourself for not stepping in and saying more."

Etien said nothing.

"Etien, you are a faithful friend. Don't punish yourself because you didn't act. You made up for your caution ten times over. You stood by Louis when the rest of the world deserted him."

"I had to," said Etien. "We were like brothers. We still are."

"I know." Bishou still held his hand. "I saw you and heard you together last night."

"I think he loves you, Bishou. I hope he does. How do you feel about him?"

"Whatever we feel is between him and me, Etien."

"How could a woman not love him?" Etien asked.

Bishou smiled, and squeezed his hand. "I have no answer to that question, *mon ami*."

"I was so frightened when I saw you wandering around town," Etien confessed. "I was afraid the whole business was starting again, a woman sneaking off to make plans against him. I didn't feel strong enough to go through it a second time."

"Once was enough, Etien," she agreed. "It won't happen again, I promise. You must learn to trust me, Etien. I know it will be hard, at first. Your conscience still punishes you."

"Yes, it does," he admitted. "I know I must—let go—enough to trust."

"So does he," she said softly.

Etien started. "I—I hadn't really thought of it like that. He is the burned child who fears the flame, is he not?"

"I may just go back home."

"I hope not," Etien replied. "At least, get a job and stay in the neighborhood. He's not made of stone." Suddenly, he smiled, a shy, sweet smile.

Bishou laughed. Gently, she kissed his cheek. "Now you must go home. Or are you going back to work?"

"I'm going home for lunch. I probably will tell Denise, you know."

"You have a treasure in her, and she in you," Bishou replied.

"I only wish the same happiness for Louis. I hope you understand," said Etien apologetically.

"I do understand. Go home. *Au revoir*, Etien."

"*Au revoir*, Bishou."

Etien left her at the université and went back out to his car. Bishou stared at the posting for a long moment. Then, she heard a woman's voice.

"Docteur Howard?"

"*Oui.*" She turned, and recognized the elder secretary. "*Bonjour*, Madame Ellis."

"I thought that might be you, Docteur." She stood beside Bishou and also regarded the job board. "Were you looking to see if there were more postings?"

"No, I was showing the advertisement to a friend."

"So I saw. That was Monsieur Campard, was it not?"

"*Oui*, Etien Campard. We were 'pen pals' before we met."

"Ah, I see." Pen pals were common here.

"I should tell you—Monsieur le Doyen is favorably disposed to having a woman on staff, and he is greatly respected by the université. He comes to us straight from the Sorbonne, you know."

"So I saw, after I researched him."

"Ah! You did? Where?"

"The université library, in America. The College for Humanities here is a school to be proud of."

"We are so new," said Mme. Ellis, "the newest of the schools, you know. The schools for sciences and technology were established first. We were almost an afterthought."

"That is sad," said Bishou. "Humanities are very important. Philosophy, literature—they make a student think about right and wrong. They make a scientist wonder about ethics. Everyone must think about how they will conduct their lives."

"I am glad to hear you say that," said Mme. Ellis. "Of course,

I do not know for certain whether they will hire you. I am not in the inner circle of these decisions."

"I understand, and thank you for your kind words."

"What are you planning to do if you don't get the job?"

Bishou smiled. "I am superstitious enough not to speak of the future."

"Do you—is it rude to ask—do you have plans to stay here nonetheless?"

"I think perhaps yes. As I told Monsieur le Doyen, this is a beautiful land, much like the Université of Virginia, where I got my doctorate."

"I think he was surprised that *une Americaine* would know so much about French universités."

"Academia is the same, almost everywhere. Harvard, Yale, Cornell, Purdue, Columbia, Duke, Notre Dame—if you go to one of them, you will be as comfortable there as you are here."

Mme. Ellis smiled. "But they do not speak French."

Bishou laughed. "Perhaps, perhaps not. After all, East Virginia University is not famous for its French-speaking population."

Mme. Ellis smiled again, and held out her hand. "*Au revoir*, Docteur, *et bonne chance*."

"*Merci*, Madame." They shook hands, and the secretary walked back to work.

Wonder of wonders, thought Bishou. *The secretaries are rooting for me. Some things are universal, after all.*

***

Bishou had walked farther than she realized. She waited at the université bus stop, and caught the bus back to Missy's. Then she strolled down the street to the pension. She saw the little white convertible, and realized guiltily that it was past three o'clock. Bishou opened the front door of the pension and stepped inside.

Louis was whiling away the time at the counter, talking to the two sisters. They were almost overwhelmed at having the millionaire in their little pension. But he was being very low-key, having a nice conversation with them about the weather and fishing and tourists. It was the ladies' reactions, rather than the sound of the door, that made him turn.

"*Bonjour*, Mademoiselle. Have you enjoyed your morning?" he asked.

"Very much, thank you."

"Do you need anything?" He glanced at her clothes, perhaps to hint that she should change from her academic outfit. "It will probably be dark before I bring you back."

"*D'accord*. I want to fetch some things from my room."

She ran up the stairs to her room, unlocked the door, went inside, and rummaged through her backpack. She pulled out a cotton summer housedress and flat shoes, and put them on. She found her cardigan, and slid her papers into a leather binder. Then she locked her room and hurried downstairs.

"I am ready."

Louis said goodbye to the sisters, and accompanied her out the door. Once in the car, he turned to her and said, "*Tu es très jolie*." His tone was familiar and personal.

"*Merci*."

"You should have nice shoes, and a sundress," he said. "Perhaps we will buy those before you leave the island."

"Perhaps," she said.

He smiled and started the car. They were driving down a grassy, green jungle road when he spoke again. "I told Etien I was not bringing you over for dinner at their place, that we were dining at my house."

"Really?"

"Really," he affirmed. "I wanted a chance to speak to you without ten thousand interruptions."

Bishou smiled. "Those boys were lively, weren't they?"

"Their parents were just as bad. Denise kept repeating herself, and Etien kept interrupting." Louis shifted gears. "I was stunned enough, without their interference. You never did explain why you came here. Except to say that you wanted to see how I was doing."

She leaned back, and closed her eyes. "Well, that was the truth."

He reached over with one hand, and touched two fingers to her cheek—a kiss of sorts. "And what else?"

"The freedom of travel, I suppose. Bat said, just get out of here for a while, and this was a good destination."

"His letter said he did not know your forwarding address."

"He merely meant I hadn't sent him a timetable. I just took things as they came."

"Did he know you were coming here?"

"Yes, he did." She sat up as they left the city and entered the greenness of the countryside. She smelled vegetation. Jungle foliage hung down at the sides of the road. Unknown animals called to each other. Beautiful birds sang in the trees. The island's two great volcanoes, covered with greenery almost to the peaks, could be seen in the distance. The sky was summery blue. "It is spring here, isn't it—well, as much spring as it becomes?"

"*Oui.*" He turned down another road, and then a third one. They drove toward a beautiful, three-story white house with elegant brass and wrought-iron railings on its balconies, and open windows everywhere. Under a large shade tree sat a table with chairs. It was a fairyland home. Louis pulled up in front of it, stopped, and shut off the engine.

"*Chez toi?*" she asked in wonder. Your home?

"*Chez moi,*" he affirmed with a smile.

"How beautiful!"

"I'm glad you like it." He got out of the car, came around to open her door, and held out a hand. She took it, and they walked hand in hand to the house.

Two ladies waited inside the front door. Louis introduced them. "My housekeeper, Bettina—"

"—and Madeleine," Bishou finished, holding out a hand to each of them. "The Campard boys told me your names. I am pleased to meet you."

Both women brightened, although they had already looked happy. "*Bienvenue*, Mademoiselle," said Bettina. Madeleine repeated the welcome.

Louis took Bishou into his salon, while the women returned to the kitchen. The furniture was a mixture of French Provincial and basket chair. Louis squatted down by a small cabinet and removed a wine bottle.

As he stood, he said, "In America, we would have cocktails. Do you think you could stand the taste of genuine French Chardonnay instead?"

"I don't know," she replied. "It's been so long."

Louis laughed, opened the bottle, and poured wine into two dainty wineglasses. They touched glasses. "To your health," he toasted her.

"And yours," she replied, taking a sip.

He motioned her to an ivory-colored stuffed chair near the matching couch. He sat on the couch.

"So. Tell me what happened with Bat."

"His fiancée was killed," said Bishou. "Her helicopter crashed."

"Her helicopter?" He was puzzled for a moment. "She was a pilot?" Then the answer struck him. "In the military."

"Yes. He had said nothing to my parents about his plans to marry, so he said nothing about her death. But his plans became dust, to use your phrase."

Louis winced. "I am sorry. And any expression of sympathy would be worse than saying nothing, so I say nothing."

"That's about it." Bishou sipped her wine. "I felt pretty helpless myself. I could only do what he wanted me to do—get out, travel, see things, take my turn now. He will take care of things at home, he told me."

"He gave you freedom, then," said Louis.

"*Oui.*"

"For how long?"

"That is the part that bothers me. We set no end date for this freedom." She set her glass on a little lamp table. A smile started to form on her lips. "I just figured out what is wrong here."

"Here?" He stared as she squatted down and slipped off his shoes. Hurriedly he set his glass beside hers and laughed as she grasped his legs and lifted them onto the couch. Now he sprawled on his own couch as he'd done on hers back in Virginia. She pulled up a footstool and sat beside him.

"There," she said. "This is how I am used to seeing you."

He was still laughing. "I have tried so hard to be correct, and you are blowing my good intentions to pieces." Louis pointed toward the floor. "Regarde, I even picked up my books from the place I usually drop them."

"I am glad to hear that you get comfortable in this salon. It is a nice room."

"I don't relax much, you know," Louis admitted. He sat up a little bit, and his smile vanished. His entire attitude changed. Louis held out his arms. "Bishou—*embrace-moi.*"

It didn't require much effort for them to wrap their arms around each other and kiss. His lips were soft and warm. To Bishou, his kiss was electric. When it ended, Bishou kissed his cheek, and then kissed his lips again.

"Ah, *oui,*" he said softly, eyes closed.

"I have wanted to do this for so long," she said.

"*Aussi.* Just to touch you, not to be *très* correct all the time. I will not lie, though, Bishou—I don't know what I want out of your friendship."

"You are honest enough to say so, Louis. I am still finding my way, too. And there is plenty of time."

Louis shook his head, and looked down at their clasped hands. "Most men my age have settled their lives by now. Me, I have dragged my name through the dirt and broken half the commandments, and come back to my cage like a whipped dog."

"There is nothing to settle tonight. This is a nice dinner, between friends."

He looked into her eyes. "Do you really mean that?"

"Of course I do."

"I hope you do, but that is not what women say. They say, 'Oh Louis, in your heart you have already made your decision.' And I almost must . . ."

He made a pushing motion with his hands, and she found herself laughing.

"Bail out," she supplied.

"*Oui*, bail out, run away. You, Bishou, you don't act like that. You say, 'Tell me more about Carola, she must have been a sketch,' and you laugh, and you mean it. You are honest with me. So I can speak of you comfortably, and my friends say, 'Oh, Louis loves this *Americaine*,' whether I do or not—because I can say your name."

Louis stroked her hands, focusing upon them. She clasped his rough hands, and said nothing.

A discreet throat-clearing from Bettina made them look up. "Dinner is served, Monsieur, Mademoiselle."

Louis slipped on his shoes, and they got to their feet.

"Oh, by the way," Bishou said in French. "Did I tell you I went to North Carolina and visited Vig and Sukey?"

Louis brightened. "*Non*! How are they? What is his place like?"

"His place is as big and cheerful as Vig and Sukey. Their children are as big and cheerful as the place."

Louis laughed as she described the enormous plantation. Bettina ducked in and out, serving the meal and refreshing their drinks. Bishou described staying overnight at their home, and how they had shown her the town.

"Oh, that meant drinks with them, and *biftek* somewhere," he laughed.

"Oh, yes, gigantic steaks, the size of an entire ox. And they conjured up a date for me, too." She raised an eyebrow.

Louis frowned. "Not Gray Jackson."

"How did you guess that?"

"He said you were a good-looking woman. He was warm for you from the start," Louis replied. "He mentioned you to me several times."

"I think he was trying to judge your reaction, because I was your interpreter and he wanted to cut in," said Bishou.

"Excuse me—'cut in'?"

"I will explain later. This is food is too good to explain now," Bishou said, taking a mouthful of chicken. "Mmm. I haven't dined this well since I left America."

"Well, thank you. I will make sure my staff knows, too."

A cloud still hung over him, though. Apparently, Louis hadn't been as oblivious as Gray Jackson thought he was. It looked as though it might have taken an effort for him to pick up his fork and continue. Bishou glanced at his face. She took another bite.

"You should come back to the United States sometime, and see other parts of it," she continued. "I admit, Virginia was a good introduction. I would enjoy showing you some of the other places I've visited. The Grand Canyon. The Mississippi River. New England. Florida. Amish country. There is so much to see in America."

"It would be nice," Louis said, "and I am a little curious. However, the tobacco business takes much of my time, and I am grateful to have it. And, if I were away, Etien—you know?"

"As if you said, Guess what, Etien you are going to the dentist daily for two weeks."

Louis laughed again. "Exactly. For Etien, it would be agony prolonged."

For dessert they had mangoes with ice cream. In France, it would have been an apple, no ice cream. *Little things change with climate*, she mused. They talked about where the ice cream was made locally, the mangoes, even the sugar syrup, while they ate.

Bettina filled their coffee cups, and they took them to the salon so she could clear the table. Louis sat again on the couch, Bishou on the ottoman. It was more intimate than the easy chair. Louis was comfortable with it, too. She hadn't realized how tense he had been until she wrestled his legs up onto the couch. Now, he was smiling and relaxed. His dark eyes danced as he recollected dining out with Vig and Sukey, and things various tobacco-men said.

"We were all like children," Louis said, "having fun together."

"All meetings should be that way," Bishou agreed.

"*Oui*. More people would come to meetings if they were that pleasant. But I should have warned you that Gray Jackson had designs on you, except that how were you to know I was not trying to take you, myself? It was an awkwardness for me."

"I understand. He said the same about you."

"*Moi*?" Louis sat up on the couch indignantly. "He is a gangster, Bishou. All this organizing? It is organized crime. He got his roots in—what you call—rumrunning, 'revenooing'—and there are still shady dealings with the American law." It was the plainest indication how Louis saw himself, not as a career criminal, but as a loner who made stupid mistakes.

"One expects that in a Southerner. It goes almost without saying."

"Does it? Now you surprise me."

"There's no Southerner who doesn't know who and where the law is, and how to get around it. That's why they are always cautious of us Yankees. We usually represent the law, or are at least very familiar with it."

"He was not cautious of you, Bishou. He spoke of your nice skin and your warm shoulders, and wondered how you would be . . ." Louis reddened.

"All right, you don't have to finish that sentence," she said, her face reddening too.

"I should hope not. But he was someone for you to guard against, Bishou, and I only hope you gave him nothing to lead him on."

Bishou regarded Louis with surprise. "You're jealous. *Mon Dieu*, Louis Dessant, you're jealous of Gray Jackson!"

"I am not jealous," said Louis defensively, the emptiest protest since time began.

"Listen to you!" she exclaimed incredulously. "What has Gray Jackson got that you haven't got? You are as jealous of him as he was of you. He couldn't wait for the bus to leave to ask me over to his hotel room."

"What?" Louis sat up. Both feet hit the floor. He uttered an expletive Bishou didn't bother translating, followed by, "He wanted you to go to bed with him?"

"Sure. Fact. Now that the 'poor little rich boy' was on his way to the airport, why couldn't I give him what I'd given you?" Bishou heard that familiar growl, and added, "And, I admit, he got slightly more than you—because when we went to the bar, I paid for his drink. You haven't let me buy you a drink yet."

"Nor will I." His cheeks were still flushed. "The idea."

"And we were both lucky neither of us yet knew that you'd purchased my cap and gown for me, Louis, or I would have had no defense against him."

He bowed his head. "I had not thought of it like that." Louis swallowed, and dropped his gaze. "Anyone would have thought you were *ma maîtresse*." My mistress. "I meant it only as a kindness."

"I knew, Louis. I understood. And damn the rest of them." His gaze came back up to her face, and she sighed, "And there are the puppy-dog eyes he spoke of, that melt all the women's hearts."

The puppy-dog look vanished immediately, replaced by one of sheer mischief. "Gray Jackson said that?"

"*Bien sûr*, and much more besides. You are jealous of each other because you are so alike."

"I don't think so."

"I do. Answer my question, then. What does Gray Jackson have that you don't have?"

"Freedom to do whatever he wants," Louis replied promptly.

"And what have you got that he doesn't have?"

"That, I do not know," Louis admitted.

"Thank God," said Bishou, and she kissed him.

She sat beside him on the couch, and kissed him again. Whether it was her forwardness that shocked him, or this was a fantasy come true, she couldn't tell, but he responded wholeheartedly.

"Ah, *oui*," he gasped at last. "*Ma* Bishou, I am crumbling." Louis pulled her closely. Two of his fingers stroked her throat, down toward her breast. He unbuttoned two buttons on her blouse. "I was a married man, you know."

"And I have never married," she said softly.

"*Tu es vierge*? Of course you are." His fingers were warm against her throat. He kissed her ear gently. "As I was once. Bishou, stay with me."

"I want to—"

"Marry me."

"You said that you did not want to make that decision." Bishou closed her eyes and clasped his hand.

"I lied. I am too lonely. Will you marry me?" Louis drew her close to him.

"*Oui*."

***

They sat together, blissfully, for quite some time, before they heard Bettina clear her throat. Bishou didn't move. Louis merely looked up at his housekeeper. "Bettina, *elle m'a dit oui*." She told me yes.

"Oh!" Bettina almost dropped the coffee cup. "*Mes felicitations*, Monsieur, Mademoiselle! I will tell Madeleine!" She ran out of the room with the dirty dishes.

"She was expecting that," Bishou observed.

"My *domestiques* are much wiser than I am," Louis replied. "I am a source of constant amusement to them."

"That is as it should be."

He smiled at her, and stroked her hair. "And you have never kept *domestiques*."

"No matter."

He nuzzled her throat. "No matter." He sighed. "I am starting all over again. I don't know what the church will allow. Suppose they will not let us marry?"

"Then we'll get a civil license."

"My thought too. And soon. You know, there are no long engagements on Réunion Island. The wedding may take place three days later."

"Three days?" she said, surprised.

"*Oui*. Where would a mail-order bride wait in the meantime? We could be married later this week."

"Then I had best tell Bat to get his tail out here, soon, if he's going to be my witness." She kissed Louis's cheek again. "After all, he was the one who said, 'Get that man, Bishou, if he's worth it.'"

"Then I owe him. And I feel I should meet your twin."

She smiled and admitted, "He asked me if you were hot. I said yes, but not for me. Now you make a liar out of me."

"As Vig would say, you snuck in through the back door. I probably would not have noticed you so much if Gray hadn't kept pointing you out to me." A thought occurred to him. "Do you think he did that on purpose?"

"He might have. Gray is a schemer."

"A good word for him. Now, though, you must contact your brother and tell him to come here."

"This is going to be expensive."

He snorted. "There speaks the graduate student. Not Dessant."

"*Mon Dieu*, Louis! You cannot pay for all this."

"Why not? I did the first time."

"And it wasn't right, then." She stroked his face. "What can I pay for, or give you, in return?"

"Well . . ." He glanced down at her hands. "There is one thing."

"And that is?"

"An American custom Sukey talked about, which I had never heard. That when lycéennes fall in love, they exchange rings."

Bishou fought hard to keep a straight face. "You want my college ring?" She remembered how he had detected her by it, from the start. She slipped it off. Between them, they found that it fit best on his left pinky finger.

Louis smiled and stroked it as if he had been given a precious jewel. *He's allowing himself to fall in love again*, Bishou thought suddenly, *I can't disturb this.*

"Now, I can take you home. If I wake up in the night and wonder if it was a dream, I will have the ring."

Bishou lifted his hands to her lips and kissed the ring finger. "This is real, Louis. It will happen."

"If it were more than a few days, it would be unbearable," he replied, "because I cannot believe it is true. I am happy, Bishou— yet this is so painful, too."

She kissed him again. "I understand. We will be very careful. We will remember that it is not the wedding that matters, it's the marriage."

"Exactly." His voice sounded husky. "I want to start over, to do it right this time. But someone is bound to say to you, 'Ah *oui, la deuxieme* Madame Dessant.'" The second Mrs. Dessant.

She smiled, and let his look of mischief seep into her own eyes. "Or I may introduce myself that way. That will fetch them."

Louis Dessant laughed. Curled up on his own couch, a ring on his finger, his bride-to-be beside him—suddenly he looked like he had reached the place that other men found naturally. Bishou let him pull her onto his lap and kiss her.

"Now I must take you back to the pension," he told her. "That will be the most difficult thing I have done this evening. I want you to stay here, but—well, I am the widower, and one of us should be *vierge* on our wedding night."

Bishou snickered. "*D'accord*. My job."

"You are a good sport."

"That ring was expensive."

He laughed again.

Chapter 16

She woke to the whistle of the *Mauritius Pride* docking. That meant it was nine A.M. Bishou sat up and looked around her hotel room. She must have just shed her clothing on her way to bed. Well, it had been a wild night. Her class ring was still gone— good, she hadn't imagined it.

She wasn't hung over. They hadn't drunk too much wine. It was high spirits of another sort. "Good gosh," she said to herself, picking up clothes from the floor. "I just agreed to marry Louis Dessant." She sat down in the hotel chair and smiled foolishly.

Oddly enough, they'd gotten back to the pension at a reasonable hour, a little before midnight—delayed, of course, by kissing in the car, somewhere along the way. Bishou laughed to herself. She couldn't have imagined she would be this happy. She had just wanted to give Louis a chance at the happiness he'd missed, and she would do all the support stuff that she and Bat had done for their own family, to keep things from being too horrible. But this wasn't turning out like that at all. There were bursts of happiness that were completely unexpected. *Maybe this is what love is all about*, Bishou mused. *And maybe even some of that passion I've spent so much time analyzing for dissertations.*

Dissertations. *Must see about the progress of that job today*, she thought, *and when they want me to do an expository lecture.* The Bible as Literature? That would be a good topic, especially in this day and age in France, where religion is so questioned. "That topic would work," she murmured.

She changed her clothes, visited the bathroom at the end of the hall, and came back to clear everything up. Louis had invited her to come to the factory around two.

The sisters waited, downstairs. "Well, Mademoiselle," Marie teased, "you got in just before Joseph barred the door last night."

"It was close," Bishou agreed good-humoredly. "We had a good time. We laughed and laughed."

They invited her behind the counter again for coffee and croissants in their own personal quarters. She told stories about Vig and Sukey and their big North Carolina plantation, and how they made Louis Dessant laugh.

"And what of you?" Eliane asked at last.

"How do you mean?" Bishou asked in return.

"Well, an evening with *un veuf réunionnais?*" A Réunion widower.

"Mademoiselle," Marie interrupted, "your ring is gone."

Bishou smiled and touched her finger to her lips. "Alas, it has gone with my heart."

Both women's eyes widened. They sat up straighter.

"Ssh, ssh, ssh! Not a word, for at least another day," Bishou said. "In the meantime, keep looking for the ring, *hein?* And you may see it."

She left them staring at each other in delight as she skipped out the door, and down the street. Bishou saw people smiling at her. Of course it showed—she was in love. Living it, not writing about it. It was going to be difficult to tamp this down, Bat-like, and apply herself to the work in hand. She glanced at herself in a shopwindow, and stopped to brush back her hair.

"Oh, I am a fool," she said to herself, still smiling. Then she hurried on.

She caught the bus to the *université*, got off at the gates, and went inside. The job announcement for the professorial position had been taken down. She entered the building for the College for the Humanities, to see if the job was hers, or someone else's. *I can take it, either way,* she told herself. *After last night, I am guaranteed to be here for the long haul.*

Bishou stepped up to the front counter, and heard her name.

"Dr. Howard!" said Mme. Ellis incredulously. "You couldn't have already received the letter. I just posted it this morning!"

"Then my friends will receive it this evening, and show it to me." She had arranged for her mail to be delivered in care of the Campards. "Can you show me the carbon copy?"

It was in the top of the secretary's correspondence folder. She pulled it out at once, somehow conveying this was as efficient an office as anything Bishou might find overseas. Bishou read it through, a request for a 7:00 P.M. time slot on Wednesday to make a presentation of her choice to a mixed audience of students and faculty, and smiled.

"Perfect," she said.

"Is this new? A public lecture?" Mme. Ellis asked.

"Are you going to come?" Bishou asked her.

"Me? To a lecture?"

Bishou's gaze had taken in the other secretaries, who were of course listening in. "Us?"

"*Bien sûr*. It is public. You might be thinking of taking a course, or sending your nieces and nephews here."

"I never thought—yes, I would like to hear you speak, especially an *Americaine*," said Mme. Ellis. "Dr. Castelle said to Monsieur le Doyen that American lecture style is different from the European style, and Dr. Rubin said, 'All the better if we want to represent the world.' "

So they had been talking about her, where the secretaries could hear.

She did not tell Mme. Ellis that, only a day or two after the lecture, her name would change. If the academic world frowned on women, it was bitter toward women who suddenly got married. How would we know, Madame, if in a year or two, you would leave us to have babies? That was the way these universities thought, just like factories. That was why Bishou had been willing to take a part-time, or adjunct, job, without the usual academic benefits or perks.

In a just-beginning field like this, the job might be a first-time, exploratory position, to see what sort of professors it conjured up—professors who were willing to take the job for the good résumé it provided, nevermind the inadequate pay and benefits. But one couldn't survive on such a job, unless it expanded over time to become a full professorship with full benefits—or the professor had a sideline that paid real money. Bishou was now in that fortunate position, and had no intention of telling them so. She would play a straight academic game with them. Her private life was none of their business. And the fact that the job ad had already been taken down showed that they were tremendously disposed in her favor.

As she climbed onto the bus, Armand greeted her with, "*Bon matin*, Mam'selle Bishou! Got your job yet?"

She paid him. "Not yet, Armand, but it looks good. Can I go to the Dessant factory with you?"

"Sure enough. It'll be a while. Got any on you?"

"For you? Always, Armand." She gave him four cigarettes. "That's where my money goes, handsome men."

"Ah, Mam'selle is in love," said Armand with a grin.

"I may as well say it, because I know it shows."

"Who is the lucky man?"

"I am not telling. You will know soon enough."

The bus driver laughed. "*Bonne chance*, missy! You will be happy."

"*Merci*. I intend to be."

"That is what makes happiness," Armand continued. "You decide to be."

Bishou was impressed. "So many people do not understand that, *mon ami*."

"And so they are unhappy, Mam'selle."

"*Bien dit*. See? You didn't need to go to *université* to learn that, did you?"

Armand laughed again. "You are wise, and it has nothing to do with *université*, Mam'selle."

"*Nous verrons*," she replied. We will see.

She dropped off the bus at the turnoff for the Dessant Cigarette factory, and walked up the driveway to the security booth. The old guard smiled at her, and she at him.

"*Bonjour*. Are you called Joel?" she asked.

"*Oui, bonjour*. And you'd be called Mam'selle Howard, *n'est-ce pas?*" He gave her a pass to the front door. There, another guard telephoned the front office.

The place was booming. The smell of fresh-cut tobacco filled the air. It was the packaging machines that made all the noise, she could see, as automatic arms dropped, belts whirled, cartons slid. Bishou watched, fascinated, until someone touched her arm. A neat young Frenchwoman stood there, and motioned toward another door. She escorted Bishou to a pair of double doors that closed behind them. The sound immediately abated.

"Whew!" said Bishou. "One doesn't realize the noise! I'm sorry. *Bonjour*. My name is Bishou Howard."

The elegant little secretary smiled. "*Bonjour*. My name is Claire Aucoeur. I am Monsieur Dessant's secretary."

"I am very pleased to meet you," said Bishou.

"And I to meet you, Mademoiselle Howard," said Claire.

As they walked along, Bishou asked her, "Did you send the teletype message for Monsieur Campard, to Virginia?"

"*Oui*, Mademoiselle," Claire admitted with a smile.

"Then you know all about me."

"I know something of you, Mademoiselle," the secretary said politely.

"That is a relief. I have great difficulty explaining myself again and again, and there is nothing more wonderful than a good secretary who doesn't need all that."

Claire smiled, opened a half-glass door that said OFFICE, and motioned her inside. It was a large institutional room with four desks, shelves, plenty of filing cabinets, and a picture of a

Dessant Cigarette package on the wall. As offices went, it was stark, with the two bosses' desks on one side of the room and the two secretaries' desks on the other. However, Bishou guessed that neither boss spent more time than necessary at those desks.

Both Etien and Louis stood up, smiling at her. Bishou kissed Louis on each cheek, then kissed Etien on each cheek. She was introduced to Anna, the other secretary, as if Bishou were any other welcome female visitor to the factory.

Etien said, "Oh, Bishou. I have a letter from the *université* that came for you in care of us—it arrived this noon. It's in my car. I'll go fetch it." He hurried off.

Louis offered to give her a tour of the offices. Bishou saw smiles pass between the two secretaries as they left the room, and observed to Louis, "You're not fooling them in the least, you know."

"Then let's not attempt to fool them." He dragged her back into the room. "Claire. Anna. *Venez.*" Smilingly, obediently, they came over to their boss. "I am not telling you a secret if I say Bishou and I are about to be married, am I?"

Both women giggled. "*Non*, Monsieur."

"There, see?" he said to Bishou, who was laughing, too. "Mademoiselle Bishou said no more secrets. So there are no secrets. Fixed."

The secretaries convulsed into laughter.

Bishou snorted, "*Les hommes!*" Men!

"We wish you the greatest happiness, Monsieur *et* Mademoiselle," Anna said.

Louis guided her through the factory, showing her the machines that cut tobacco, made cigarettes, packaged them, and boxed them. He showed her where the new cotton-filter equipment was being installed, to remove seeds from the cotton bolls, pack it into filters, and package cigarettes similarly. It was a huge operation. Bishou had a hard time conceiving of the amount of tobacco that this plant handled daily, the number of crates of cartons of cigarettes it shipped.

"It must blind you after a while."

"It is very absorbing," Louis agreed. "Etien finds it sometimes overwhelming, and must step away and look back at it from a distance."

"Ah, here you are!" Etien caught up with them. He handed her the envelope. "Is this about the *université* job, then?"

"*Université* job?" asked Louis blankly.

"*Oui,* Bishou had applied for a position as literature professor at UFOI," Etien told him. "I met her in front of the gates, yesterday." Not much of a lie, better than the whole truth.

Bishou opened the envelope and read the same letter she had read as a carbon copy. However, there was a handwritten enclosure. She wondered if the secretary had known about this. A little envelope labeled "Dr. Howard *et Invite*"—Dr. Howard and Guest—accompanied a note that read:

> *Dr. Howard,*
> *I hope you can spare the time, after your presentation, to join us at the University Library for the opening of the newly established Clemenceau Rare Books Room. There is a reception, which would, I hope, give faculty and staff an informal opportunity to meet you. It is inspiring to our women students to meet a woman with your achievements. I hope you and your guest will join us.*
> *Sincerely,*
> *Dr. Serge Michelin, President d'UFOI*

The engraved invitation, her ticket, was enclosed.

"So," said Louis, "still, your brain wants academia?"

"If I do not use it, I will lose it," Bishou replied, thoughtfully frowning at the enclosure.

"May I see that?" Louis asked, in his mildest voice.

Instinct told her this was not a time to say no. She handed over the letter and the enclosures to him. He read carefully, with Etien standing by, and then folded the papers and put them back in their places. She had forgotten how careful and neat he was.

"So—you give a sample lecture? Is that it?" Louis asked Bishou.

She nodded, wondering how he was going to take this.

He smiled. "It is sensible. They cannot walk in on one of your lectures, like I did."

"I know. They must see me at work. It is a very stressful time, though, for a professorial candidate."

"I hate to make it more stressful by becoming the Guest," said Louis.

"I expected that," said Bishou.

"*Bien sûr*. If your job depends on the lecture of Wednesday, knowing you will be married on the same Friday, you are either going to need an escort or an ambulance attendant," said her fiancé.

"Ambulance attendant," she sighed, putting her arms around his neck.

"All Americans are nuts," Louis said, holding her, and Etien dissolved into laughter.

Chapter 17

Denise Campard laughed and laughed. "And then what happened?"

"Then we got on the telephone, and made a transatlantic call to Bat Howard," Louis told her, as they ate mango ice cream in the little living room. "My *secrétaire* Claire took notes, so she would know how to do it next time, but Bishou did the actual telephoning."

Bishou took up the tale. "When he answered, 'Howard residence' I said, 'Got your bags packed, brother?' Bat said, 'Sure enough, the black-and-whites are ready to go.' He told me that he was coming, maybe with one of my brothers or both. He'd heard from East Virginia University that they'd been asked for references for me from UFOI. I asked him what his plans were, and he said Logan to Orly to Garros. And they would see me when they saw me."

"Claire can tell us when that will be," Louis interjected.

"*Bat* can tell us when that will be," Bishou answered. "He is rather independent-minded."

"*Quelle surprise*, when you are so docile," teased Louis. "I must make sure there is a clause about 'obedience' in that marriage vow."

"Yes, you must," she said, looking at him seriously.

"Hah!" Louis recognized genuine commitment before witnesses when he heard it. "And would you dare to say it?"

"I am marrying a tobacco-man. I must take risks."

Louis smiled gently and hugged her.

"Do your brothers have passports?" Denise wanted to know.

"*Oui*. Our parents were professors. We traveled to many places. Also, because we are of mixed parentage—Canadian and American—we have dual citizenship, and need documentation."

"And now that you have reached your majority, you have declared yourself?" Etien asked.

"American. As my brother has done. The governments are tightening up the rules on that, but I think Andy and Gerry will eventually choose to be American, too. We have been to Canada only to visit relatives at the big universities. My younger brothers won't miss having Canadian citizenship."

"Although it is a way to avoid military service, in your country," Etien observed thoughtfully.

"True. The one who first qualified for an exemption is the one who gave it up first."

"Semper fi," Louis murmured.

She nodded. "Semper fi. Always faithful. The United States Marines. It was very hard on Bat, but he worked through it—or up to it."

"And then, in turn, he taught the soldiers. Sergeant Major."

She smiled, agreeing, "And then he taught them."

"Teachers all," said Denise.

***

They were driving back into town, in the dark, when Louis pulled over to the side of the road and shut off the ignition. It surprised Bishou. They had gone many miles in complete silence.

She couldn't see his face in this utter African darkness. "What's wrong?"

"Many things," said Louis. "Maybe it is what they call cold feet, *hein?*"

"Well, then, let us warm up the cold feet," she said agreeably.

"How you say that. That is one of the things."

"I'm not sure I understand."

"This is not . . ." Louis began again. "This is not love as I know it, Bishou. I keep waiting for the pain. I have learned that love is pain."

"And where there is no pain, there is no love?" she asked softly.

"Carola took everything from me. She poisoned me because she couldn't bear to see how much I hurt, so ashamed and disgraced." His voice was full of emotion. "And when I realized what she did, I said—"

"'I know what you are doing. Fill it up. I can't bear to live without you.' Yes, I know."

There was a long silence in the darkness.

He said, "That was when she burst into tears and said to me, 'I finally understand that love is always pain.'"

"But she did not refill your glass."

"*Non.*" Bishou knew that Louis was crying. "We ran away into the snow, into the darkness, together. And we had no hope. None at all." She heard him hit the steering wheel. "What am I doing?"

"Not what am I doing. What are *we* doing," she said.

"You, Bishou! You don't know. You are like a child, like I was then. To be seduced, to learn how to be seduced, to be miserable every moment you are with your lover, and miserable without her! Not to kill her, but to kill *for* her, and live with that the rest of one's life!"

Bishou reached out, and found his shoulders in the darkness. She wrapped one arm around his shoulder. She spoke steadily. "*Non, vrai,* those are things I do not know. But I know how shattering it is to see a mother's body and spirit destroyed in a ridiculous accident, and a father's mind ruined as a result, and see all hope of a normal family life, of ordinary happiness, vanish. No father, no mother, no true family. And we stupid children, desperate to keep our family together, despite all odds."

She heard him sniff. "What you are saying is that I am not the only wreck adrift in this storm."

"*Bien sûr.*"

"Oh, hell, where is my handkerchief?" She heard him blow his nose. "You don't want this horrid thing, do you?"

"I've got one in my purse if I need it."

"I will bet you don't."

"I will bet I do." She felt around the car floor. "Hey, where's my purse?"

"Ah-hah!"

"You skunk, you've nicked my purse!"

"I will win this bet if I have to sit on your purse all the way to town. Oo-hoo! Mam'selle, watch where you place those hands. I am an engaged man."

***

The ship's horn sounded later in the morning. *That's right*, she thought, *it's Saturday. I'm finally adjusting to day and night on the island.*

Bishou had slept the night through, and hadn't felt the need for an afternoon nap, even with the seductive noon-to-two siesta hours calling to her. When she came downstairs, later than usual, Eliane and Marie were waiting for her. They had knowing looks on their narrow French faces as they motioned her over to the counter.

"*Qu'est-ce que j'ai fait?*" she asked. What did I do?

"*Rien, rien.*" Nothing, nothing.

Marie pulled her by the arm, and Eliane counted cash out of the drawer.

Bishou stared. "I don't understand."

"It is a refund. You have overpaid for your room."

"What? How can that be?"

"Your room was paid for by the man with your ring on his finger."

"Ah, *non!*" she exclaimed. She covered her face with her hands. "He is being too kind."

"He is behaving like your husband," the elder sister scolded, "even if you are not yet married."

"Oh, it looks so improper."

Both women laughed. "Bishou," Marie chided, "how can you speak of 'improper' on Réunion Island? Don't you know how the first women arrived here? They were bought and paid for. This is only a room."

They laughed at her crimson face, and brought her behind the counter to their little nest for coffee and croissants.

"When did he come here?" she asked them.

"Early this morning, while you still slept, and said not to wake you. But then I said, 'Ah! The ring!' and the whole story came out," Eliane replied. "And you said nothing when we told you his history. You should have your ears boxed, young lady."

"Don't be hard on me," Bishou returned. "I didn't want to damage his reputation even more. When I first arrived here, I only thought I would see him, say hello, and see how he felt about me."

"Well, I think that question has been answered," said Eliane.

"Do you love him?" Marie pressed.

"I am a fool for him," Bishou admitted. "Only he brought me to this island." She counted the money they had pressed back in her hands—a week's lodgings. "What shall I do with this money?"

"Spend it foolishly," Marie advised with a smile.

Chapter 18

She bought the sundress she had been admiring in the store window. While she purchased it, Bishou discussed underwear with the woman manager, particularly for a full-figured girl such as herself—not a subject she got much help on at home.

"Your figure is not as flat-chested French as it is voluptuous African," the woman advised with a smile. "While you are vacationing here, in this climate, you might adopt looser clothing, for comfort. It is very easy to get rashes and skin infections, unless one is careful."

"Unfortunately," said Bishou, "I must attend several more formal functions, and I must look—forgive the term—Western."

Madame Ross, obviously a Frenchwoman, merely laughed. "Buy your casual clothes here, and let Nadine's shop fit you formally. Not the flounced skirts that are now the rage, Mademoiselle. They go well on small-chested women. You need fitted, well-tailored, below-the-knee skirts on your party dresses, with tight shoulders and a tight bodice, showing the curves of your breasts—everything that is totally against *la mode*. But you will look most elegant in them."

"I am so grateful for your advice," Bishou replied fervently, paying cash for her purchases. "I grew up in a house full of brothers. I have only a vague idea what is right or wrong in fashion, and I don't want to embarrass anyone. But certainly none of the men will come shopping with me, to tell me what they like or don't like."

Madame Ross laughed again, both in appreciation of the compliment and the cash. "Remember that your figure is not that of France, but that of Réunion, and you will be all right."

Her words stayed with Bishou. Not of France, but that of Réunion. She moved next door to Nadine's—the place she had mistaken for a bridal shop—and entered. A number of almost-finished, rather nice dresses hung on racks. *These dresses are tiny,* she thought. *For teeny, flat-chested Frenchwomen. Is that what Carola was?*

She was ignored by the two saleswomen in the store as they chatted with another couple, obviously about to get married. From the corner of her eye, Bishou saw white dresses on another rack, with veils piled nearby, looking tediously conventional. Except the trains—the trains on these dresses seemed miles long, shimmed up behind each dress like a caboose. Bishou smiled to herself and shook her head.

She examined the colored dresses on another rack, and was struck by a beautiful blue fabric that she couldn't name—not exactly cotton, but not silk or satin, either. Bishou wondered if it was a local fabric. Both saleswomen were helping the couple, and Bishou felt intimidated, for the first time. Why was it that she could face the fiercest secretary, but was intimidated by a saleswoman in a dress shop?

"*Pardonnez-moi,*" she said to a saleswoman, who barely stopped speaking to the other customers to give her an icy stare. "Forgive me," Bishou continued humbly, "but Madame Ross referred me to you for assistance with a formal dress. Is there someone who could help me?"

"You can wait your turn, Madame," the saleswoman said coldly, turning her back upon her.

"Brrr! I suppose I can," said Bishou with a mock shiver and left the store.

She went back to Madame Ross, who looked up in surprise as she entered her shop once again.

"I have been told off, in the best Parisian fashion," Bishou said to the manager, who stifled a smile.

"They are *très* correct," Mme. Ross admitted. Very correct. "And you are . . ." Madame hazarded a guess, "not patient, and not Parisian."

"*Non, je suis Americaine.*"

"Ah, an impatient *Americaine* from a houseful of boys, who likes the African styles but must wear European ones. And do you have a name, Mademoiselle?"

"Oh, *mes apologies. Je m'appelle* Bishou."

"*Bonjour*, Mademoiselle Bishou." Mme. Ross folded her elegant hands on her little countertop, and looked amused. She had pretty blond hair, longish but held up in a way Bishou only wished she knew how to mimic. "Now. In your brief time in Nadine's shop, did you see anything you particularly liked?"

Bishou realized this trip was completely demoralizing her. "I am ready to run away, Madame. I understand now why men run in terror from shopping trips."

"Frightened by one saleswoman?" Mme. Ross placed her hand on one of Bishou's. "You are a tomboy, aren't you?"

"I suppose so," Bishou admitted.

"And why are you standing your ground, now?" Mme. Ross asked shrewdly.

"All right," Bishou confessed. "I want a special dress for a special man."

"I see." Madame seemed more amused than convinced.

"Madame Ross," said Bishou earnestly, "I have camped on a Vermont mountainside in snow and ice, with winds raging about me, at temperatures of thirty degrees below zero. I have ridden mules in the Grand Canyon, and traced the path of the Canadian Voyageurs by canoe. But nothing frightens me like that dress shop. Will you come with me, if I pay you to be my guide?"

"*Ma petite*," said the elegant little owner of the casual dress shop, "I will come with you for nothing. You appear the same age as my own daughter. She is twenty-eight."

"So am I. But you do not look old enough to have a daughter that age. I was just thinking how young and beautiful you are."

"You flatter me. My little Alicie is studying in Paris, at the École du Louvre. At this rate, I may never see her interested in buying a beautiful dress for a special man. Come." Mme. Ross clasped her hand. "We go to Nadine's. Watch things here, Ceci."

"Oui, Madame." The Creole shop assistant giggled.

Mme. Ross stepped inside the shop next door, with Bishou behind her. Together they walked over to the rack of colored dresses. The saleswomen looked up at them sharply, and returned to their important customers—although it was obvious they had recognized Mme. Ross and were keeping a cautious eye on her.

Bishou showed her the blue dress. "I don't know this fabric."

"A silk-cotton combination, and rather nice. You have a good eye," Mme. Ross said approvingly. "And this style, yes, this is exactly what I meant. *Venez.* Their dressing rooms are over here, and we can look in the mirror in the back room." She took down the hanger, and moved to the back without consulting either saleswoman. Bishou followed meekly.

"Now, slip into one of the booths and put it on, then come out and let me see. Your underwear will show, but no matter. You'll need new underwear, anyway, for these types of dresses."

"*Mon Dieu!*" said Bishou, "I can't even get them to fit a dress on me. Do you think they'll fit lingerie?"

"I will do it. For that, I will charge." Mme. Ross smiled wryly. "Remember, the special man."

"*Je me souviens.*" Bishou entered the booth, undressed, and realized that the blue dress hooked—not zipped—up the back. "This has no zippers!"

"Zippers are so American," said Mme. Ross. "Come out here and I will hook you up."

Bishou stepped out of the booth and into a bare backroom with empty tables and a cheval mirror. Nonetheless, she felt like Cinderella. She stared in the mirror while Mme. Ross hooked and pulled. Bishou stood on tiptoe before the mirror.

"Yes," said Mme. Ross, interpreting her move, "it requires high heels. But it does look elegant. And it is sized for you."

"I know. I was surprised. Most of those dresses are so tiny."

"Compared to you, many Frenchwomen are tiny. You are a healthy, well-exercised *Americaine.*"

"How are you doing, Madame Ross?" said a strident voice. The cold-eyed saleswoman regarded Bishou.

"Things go well, thank you, Madame Nadine," Mme. Ross replied. "Allow me to introduce Mademoiselle Bishou, who bought some things at my shop and then realized she needed more formal clothing as well." Mme. Ross's tone was brisk, courteous, and professional, Bishou realized approvingly.

"*Bonjour*, Mademoiselle." Nadine stepped into the area, and eyed the dress. "Did I hear Mme. Ross say that you are *Americaine?*"

"*Oui*, Madame."

"And you are visiting the island?" Being American was obviously not a point in Bishou's favor.

"*Non*, Madame, I will be living here."

The questions came like bullets. "Do you have a job here, or are you getting married?"

"*Oui, et oui.*"

"Explain, please."

Bishou reined in her temper. "Yes, I have a job here, and yes, I am getting married."

"Change back into your own clothes, please," Mme. Nadine demanded.

Bishou pulled the curtain shut, and felt the heat of her face. She could hear Mme. Ross murmuring to Nadine, and caught the words, "She paid cash. She is not *une pauvre*, Nadine." Not a pauper.

"I am not a dressmaker to American working girls, or rich Americans," was the haughty reply, "nor will I be. The women of France and Réunion Island, these are for whom I make my fashions."

Bishou changed her clothes and opened the curtain, aware that her face was still red with anger. She laid the blue dress upon a worktable. "This is very nice fabric, it is comfortable, and the dress is well-designed."

"Do you want to have a fitting, then?" Mme. Nadine demanded, almost unpleasantly.

"By no means," Bishou replied, looking her in the eye. Then she turned to Mme. Ross. "I am sorry to embarrass you, Madame. I thought that my discomfort was due to my ignorance. The ignorance, alas, was not mine. *Au revoir.*" She gathered up her purse and other parcels, and left the shop.

And almost cannoned into a gentleman in the street.

"Whoa!" said Louis Dessant, grasping her in surprise, "*Gardes-toi*, Bishou." Then he saw the look on her face. "What is the matter?"

"I hate shopping for women's clothes," she growled.

"So do I," he quipped. Louis scooped the packages out of her arms. "What are these? Réunion fashions?"

"Somewhat. There would be more if it weren't for chauvinistic, pig-headed anti-Americans."

"Ah. That was Nadine?"

"You knew?"

"I'd heard it mentioned in passing. But that is only for w-wedding dresses, and . . ."
Louis halted, his arms full of parcels. "Oh."

"*Non.*" She answered the question he did not ask. "I was just looking for a nice dress for the *université* reception, and got snubbed in the grand style."

His car was parked across the street. He opened the trunk and dumped in the packages, willy-nilly. Right now, she didn't really care. She saw a picnic basket in the trunk, and glanced at him questioningly.

Louis closed the trunk, and smiled at her. "I came looking for you because the ladies at the pension told me you had gone downtown. I thought we would tour the coast road. Bettina and Madeleine made us a picnic lunch for later. *D'accord?*"

Bishou smiled up at him, and her bad mood disappeared. "*D'accord*. I hope there's no mayonnaise in those sandwiches."

"What do you take me for? It's fruit, cheese, and peasant bread. There is red wine, but it is quite all right at room temperature—or car-trunk temperature. *Viens*."

"One more thing." She took his hand.

"Oh *mon Dieu non*, don't drag me into a woman's dress shop."

"*Non, non*, not you, nor me either. I just want you to look in a shop window."

"I can bear that," he admitted, and allowed her to lead him to the shoe store.

"Now," she said. "Which shoes did you have in mind for me? Just point."

With his dark eyes showing that he expected a bad reaction, Louis pointed to a pair of tiny high heels that might have fitted Cendrillon nicely, but were nothing like her normal style.

Bishou merely sighed, said, "I thought so," and disappeared into the shop.

A waiting shoe salesman was smiling at her as she entered the otherwise-unoccupied shop. "Is that Monsieur Dessant?" he asked.

"Certainly it is," she answered. "Do you have those shoes in my size?"

The beaming salesman obligingly measured her feet, disappeared into the back of the store, and returned in a moment with the shoes. She slipped them on, and stood up. Immediately she felt four inches taller.

"Oh, my," she said, and the salesman's smile broadened.

"They might take practice, Mademoiselle," he told her.

"I think they will," she agreed. "And also, a pair of casual shoes, those cloth ones with the rope soles, if you have them in my size."

He glowed at two sales on a slow day, wrapped up the packages, and was rewarded with a cash payment. "*Merci*, Mademoiselle . . . ?"

"Madame Bishou," she supplied her name, and he made out the receipt as such.

She emerged from the shop to see Mme. Nadine, of all people, chatting with Louis, while he plainly looked like he wished to be elsewhere. Mme. Ross and her assistant watched from the door of her shop. Likewise, others along the street had emerged to see the notorious, reclusive Louis Dessant in daylight. He spotted Bishou with evident relief, and swooped down upon her to seize her packages.

"Au revoir, Madame," he said hurriedly to Nadine, and then to Bishou, "*Tu es prêt?*" as informally as possible, as emphasis.

"*Oui, cherie, je suis prêt.*"

She had never before called him darling. He dumped the shoes into the trunk with the rest of the packages. Louis did not raise dust, nor burn rubber, getting out of town, but the intention was there.

"*Nom de nom!*" Bishou exclaimed. "How do you ever go shopping?"

"I send Bettina," he said sourly. "It takes half the day for me to get a haircut and my shoes shined."

"I should show you this," she said, as he slowed down to a reasonable speed. "It's my first receipt given to Madame Bishou."

"Put it in the glove box," he told her. "We'll add it to our wedding album."

"Do we have one?"

"We will."

Chapter 19

Louis drove through little coastal fishing hamlets and into the countryside again, gaining altitude as they traveled around the coast. At last, he turned off the road into a grassy area where a steady breeze blew. From here they had a magnificent view of the Indian Ocean.

Louis pulled a blanket out of the trunk, as well as the picnic basket. Together they laid out the blanket on a grassy meadow near the car. Bishou watched, amused, as Louis unpacked the basket. Bread and cheese and fruit, sure enough. A bottle of wine, with a corkscrew and two glasses. Napkins and butter knives and a cheese slicer. It was a genuine French picnic. She sat, docile and amused, and allowed him to organize everything.

"I must ask you," he said, as he sat down at last to eat and drink, "if you will accompany me to church on Sunday. I do not know if Père Reynaud will have time to speak to us afterward, but it might be good if we were both there. He must tell us *oui ou non*, if we can be married Friday in the church, or if we must choose the Prefecture Office instead."

"Who gave you permission to travel to America?"

"The Prefecture." Louis concentrated on his bread and cheese and did not look her in the eye. "As I said, I have not yet made things right with the Church. The Père owes me nothing, truly, and I have not asked forgiveness."

"Forgiveness?" she said in surprise. "For what?"

He shook his head and waved away her words. "I murdered someone, *ma cherie*. Nothing takes away that sin."

"Did Père Reynaud marry you?"

"Oui."

"Was there premarriage counseling, what they call pre-Cana?"

"*Non.*"

"Then, Louis, how can you—"

He cut her off. "This is Réunion, Bishou! That's all fine to talk, in France or in America. But not where a wife comes on a boat, alone, to bed with a strange man she had met only in correspondence. It is no more his fault than mine that we didn't understand why the wedding band didn't fit her, why she left me no notes, why she had no messages from family, why she didn't even have her own rosary—because she would have to open the trunk that was not hers, to look for one."

"*D'accord, d'accord,*" she said, in a conciliatory tone. "I understand."

"Do you? It took me years to understand."

His voice was sharp, and he drank the wine as though he needed it to calm his emotions. She understood the gesture, having seen Bat do the same with many a beer. She placed her hand over the hand that held the glass, and guided it down to the basket. His expression and voice gentled.

"No handwriting except her signature on the bank forms, so I could not compare it with the letters. Family photographs in the trunk, none of her. A ring that was sized for someone else."

"You have my ring," she said gently. She grasped his left hand, the hand with the ring.

"That," he began again, "is part of the reason I wanted it. To feel it. It is real."

His features showed pain, as she lifted his hand to her lips and kissed it. He clasped her hand.

"What upset you? Thinking about visiting the church?" Bishou asked. She wanted to bring this discussion down to its roots.

"*Oui.* It brought back so many bad memories. I almost would rather have a registry-office marriage, except . . . I must see if I can fight this battle."

"You do not fight it alone, Louis."

"Oh, Bishou." He gathered both her hands in his, and looked earnestly into her eyes. "You could go anywhere and do anything, with any other man. I am the problem. Don't you think I know that by now?"

"Anywhere and do anything, hmm?"

"You are strong. You are intelligent. You get your own money; you are not some man's parasite."

"Then—if I am all that—why am I here?"

He was silent.

She persisted, "Why am I here, Louis?"

Silence. He stared at their clasped hands, not at her face.

"Tell me. You must know." Bishou felt his grip tighten, and saw the tension in his lips.

Louis closed his eyes. He shook his head slightly. He did not know, or—more likely—he needed to hear her say it.

Quite clearly, with her grip firm, she said, "I am here because I love you with all my heart, Louis. *Je t'aime.*"

Barely loud enough for her to hear, Louis mumbled, "She never called me *cheri.*"

"Did she call you *mon amour?*" My love.

"*Non.*"

"Or *mon treasor?*" My treasure.

She saw a smile break through. "*Non.*"

"*Bon.* The good names are left for me." Bishou kissed his hands. "*Mon cheri.*" Kiss. "*Mon amour.*" Kiss. "*Mon treasor.*" Kiss.

His smile returned. Bishou almost expected him to protest that she was teasing him, but he did not. *He really needs this*, she thought, *a demonstration of my love.* Here, seated on the blanket, hands entwined, Louis Dessant was finally hearing words he desperately wanted to hear.

"What a dream world this is," Bishou mused. "A French picnic on a beautiful island, with an attractive, sexy man, all the world and time."

"Soon to be your husband," Louis added, still smiling.

"What joy," she agreed.

He scooped everything back in the basket, brushed crumbs from the blanket, and slipped off his jacket. He rolled it into a pillow for himself, and lay back. He hadn't worn a tie, his discreet concession to Saturday casual. Bishou realized that the shirt he had on was the same one he had worn that day when they visited the tobacco plantations with the American conventioneers.

"I remember that shirt."

"You liked it. That is why I wore it."

"It was not the shirt," she admitted, "but what was in the shirt."

With his head pillowed on the jacket, he raised a dark eyebrow in question.

"It was so hot that day," she explained. "You were falling asleep from the heat. Watching you, asleep beside me, I fought the greatest temptations I have ever faced."

"And what did you desire that day? Show me." He shut his eyes.

She realized he was deliberately seducing her. She loosened the cuffs of his silk shirt with the little colored squares, and rolled up each cuff a couple of turns. Her hands stroked the bronzed forearms, a man's forearms. She leaned over him and unbuttoned one, two, three shirt buttons, from the collar down. She stroked his jaw, his throat, his lips—felt his lips kiss her fingers—and gently stroked down his chin and throat, toward his unbuttoned shirt. Her fingers stroked his chest—no, no undershirt—and she bent and kissed the place where she had stroked, smelling a slight scent of cologne.

His eyes still closed blissfully, he sighed, "Ah, ah *oui*."

Bishou caught her breath, startled by a powerful emotion that she had never felt. "Louis," she sobbed. "Someone to love me. Someone to keep me from being alone forever. I just don't want to be alone all my life. It hurts so much. I'm sorry. I didn't mean to drop this load on you. I wanted to be strong, for your sake."

"Pfah," said Louis softly. "Don't you think I know? How many Saturday nights have I spent in my darkened front room, drink in hand, watching car lights go down the roads? Listening to people happily calling to each other? And aching, wishing I was one of them? Knowing I must stay home, keep my reputation tres correct? Why do you think they call us white men *zoreils*, cherie? Because we listen helplessly. It is all we can do. Listen, and ache inside." He wrapped his arms around her firmly. "Love given freely, to dispel loneliness, is the greatest gift. But—it is a horrible feeling, if one knows it is a bond of slavery."

She spoke to his ear and throat, not moving her head. "You knew this would happen to me."

"*Non*. But I understood when it did, *ma* Bishou." His arms still gripped her body. "You are only learning what I learned. But how could I have explained that to you?"

"And other men have learned this as well?"

"*Oui*. And, thank God, they were merciful to me when I had fallen."

Bishou saw a glimpse of this unspoken world, a world that Louis and other men shared, that had no place on any map or church roll. *There but for the grace of God go I. Please, Lord, give me to a woman who won't make me a slave in hell. Please, instead, make me petted and loved. In either case, I will give everything to her.*

That, thought Bishou, *is passion.*

"*Qu'est-ce que tu regardes?*"

"*Un bel visage*," she answered.

"Hah, there is no handsome face here, only mine."

"An attractive one, then." She watched his brown eyes open suddenly, as they always did—a trick she suspected he learned in prison. "I wonder if you know you are handsome, and only want to hear me say it."

He laughed. "*Non*. It is nice to hear, even if untrue. I know that women have said I have nice eyes, though."

"Oh, *oui*. They are the first thing I noticed about you, the first thing that made me think, *Wow*."

"Really?" Now there was a light in his eyes that was not a trick of the sun. "In that classroom?"

"You remember that day. I thought your glance was only surprise that I was not a man."

"Well, that too. 'Bishou' is not a feminine name. And you may say it means 'unexpected,' but I have not found that in any dictionary."

"Oh? You looked?" At his blush of admission, she laughed. "I will tell you a secret, if you promise not to share."

"I promise."

"My name is Japanese."

"What?" He burst into laughter, and sat up.

"My father found it in his studies. It is the character in drama who is the unexpected love interest, and who often has the sympathy of the audience. The hero often wins the girl—or the boy—away from the angst-ridden main character, just by being there and being himself or herself."

"Your father is a wise man," said Louis.

"Yes, he is. But often the Bishou doesn't get the girl—or the boy. He just provides contrast for the main characters."

"But sometimes she does, *hein*?" Louis smiled and stroked her hair.

"Sometimes," she admitted. "If she is very lucky."

Louis kissed her cheek.

Suddenly, there was a dreadful grinding sound in the air, the sound of a large vehicle downshifting up a steep road. Louis jumped. "Oh, hell," he said. "It's the tour autobus. Have I parked far enough off the road? I don't want to get sideswiped."

"You're fine. You're practically in the meadow." Bishou patted the blanket and watched the ancient double-decker bus chug into view. "Come on, don't worry. Probably seeing the famous Louis Dessant picnicking with his fiancée will be the highlight of their trip."

"*Dieu m'en garde.*" God help me. Louis waved insincerely as the bus hove into sight, every camera focused upon them.

Bishou snickered. "They probably just want photos of idyllic picnickers. They don't know who we are."

A loudspeaker from the bus pealed, "*Bonjour*, Monsieur Dessant. *Bonjour*, Mademoiselle Bishou." The bus ground to a deafening halt. Ostensibly it was for the view, or to meet the local residents, but it was probably for the engine to cool.

"I wish I'd taken that bet," said Louis. He stood with his jacket under his arm to greet the bus. "*Viens, cherie.* They even knew your name, God knows how."

They approached the bus together, where a smiling tour guide introduced them to the people on the bus and the tourists to them. Monsieur Dessant of Dessant Cigarettes, and his fiancée, Mademoiselle Bishou. Louis and Bishou asked where the people were from—which turned out to be everywhere from Lyons to Cairo—and welcomed them, playing the gracious hosts of the island.

The bus driver was looking at Bishou with a twinkle in his eye. She was sure she didn't know him. But she reached into her purse and pulled out four Dessants and gave them to him.

"Who are you related to?" she asked.

"Papa Armand," he said with a smile. "*Merci*, Mam'selle Bishou."

The white and very French tour guide had been chatting with Louis, but saw the exchange between Bishou and the driver, and smiled. "Your name is already known in our community, Mademoiselle Bishou. Welcome to Réunion, and congratulations on your upcoming marriage."

"*Merci.* I am most fortunate. I have a wonderful fiancé, and I've made good friends here."

They chatted a few moments longer, bade the tourists farewell, and stepped off the bus. The driver ground gears and the bus rattled on its way.

"Well," said Louis, "when you get caught out on moments like this, you have the royal style, for certain."

"So do you."

"I've been caught before."

"What, making out with girls on the coast road?"

A mischievous look appeared in his dark eyes. "I am not telling."

"Ah! Are you saying I must force the admission from you, later?"

"Perhaps, perhaps not. At any rate, I am looking forward to it. How do you know the bus drivers so well?"

"I think I've already met about half the Creoles in Saint-Denis. I rather like them."

"I'm glad. Sometimes, they are the true *réunionnais*."

"*Bien dit.*" Well said. "And, as Madame Ross pointed out to me, I don't have the tiny figure of a Frenchwoman—I have the more African figure of a *réunionnais*."

"*Comment?*" He stared at her. "How so?"

"My hips, my chest, even my face. I am a well-fed, well-exercised *Americaine*."

As they walked back to his car, Louis said, "Well, so I also thought. Strange. I thought of you as *réunionnais*. It hadn't occurred to me what that meant."

Bishou got in the white convertible, and he shut the door. She heard the thud of the trunk as he deposited the basket and blanket inside. Then he took the driver's seat. "You, too, are *réunionnais*, Louis. Not French."

"More and more," he agreed. "It is considered bad taste to go native, but—France has not been kind to me."

Bishou realized that was probably a dreadful admission for him to make. She touched his arm. "This island is our home."

"*Oui.* This island is our home."

Louis started the car, and began the drive down the coast road. He rummaged through his pockets, found a pack of cigarettes, extracted one and lit it with one hand. "You will need Dessants by the carton, then, as little gratuities." He drew on the cigarette, and passed it to her. Not yet married, and they had these married habits in place.

She took a couple of puffs, and passed it back. "*Oui*. They are better than money, much better. It is like Maman passing out cookies."

Louis laughed. "I am Papa, passing out cigarettes?"

"*Oui*, Papa, you are."

Again, he laughed, and downshifted to tackle the next hill. Bishou leaned back to feel the sun on her face, and thought, *Yes, I am in Paradise.*